The God Squad

in an episode of:
MISSION HIM-POSSIBLE
The Giant Slayers

Darlene Laney

Halo
PUBLISHING
INTERNATIONAL

Scripture taken from the New King James Version.

No part of this book may be reproduced in any manner without the
written consent of the publisher except for brief excerpts in critical
reviews or articles.

ISBN: 978-1-61244-721-6
Library of Congress Control Number: 2019930619

Printed in the United States of America

Halo Publishing International
1100 NW Loop 410
Suite 700 - 176
San Antonio, Texas 78213
1-877-705-9647
www.halopublishing.com
contact@halopublishing.com

This book is dedicated to all the girls attending the Color Me Beautiful Etiquette and Social Skills Development Program, past and present.

Your courage to be authentically you in such a culturally, as well as religiously diverse, world left me in awe. Like the God Squad, you are all a part of a very elite and specialized group of girls, that hearing the call, having received instruction and training, are going forth and representing to others God's good, acceptable, and perfect will for you, His daughters.

Alexis Ramirez and Ty for being the Ms. Fosters that helped to mentor, empower, teach, and support the girls that participated in the program.

Special thank you, Saria for your courage to be you-niquely, you and inspiring all around you to embrace and celebrate their own uniqueness. Grace, for showing us all what it is to be gracious in the most difficult situations.

And, to the girls at Vinland Elementary and Rowell Elementary that participated in the Girl Power Program sponsored by the Fresno Unified School District. I applaud you for your efforts in taking on a mentor/leadership role in your schools and like the God Squad serve as role models to all girls.

I applaud you!

Contents

Hi! I'm Angel. So glad you could join us for this episode of Mission Him-Possible – the Giant Slayers!

Introduction

I 've been selected to be your narrator and the leader of this mission. Oh, I'm sorry, what's a narrator? A narrator is a person that gives an account or tells the story. So that's what I will be doing. Making comments about the story from the way I see things.

Ms. Foster, that's my mentor and counselor, thought it would be good for me to introduce you to this episode because I have had a real-life experience with this subject...bullying.

It's challenging being a tween or teen these days. There is a lot we're learning and experiencing. Sometimes, we even feel pressured to do things that well we are uncomfortable doing but to look good or be accepted, you know, being cool, we go along with it.

Every day we are presented with situations that help us discover the person we are becoming. We have a lot on our heads trying to figure out who we really are; what we want to do, what we choose to believe, who our friends should be and of course, what to wear or not wear. So many decisions!

Sometimes, the decisions we make about the person we want to be, the clothes we wear to express our style, or those things that are part of our heritage; like skin color, hair and eye color, or freckles cause us to stand out from the others.

It's tough enough going through all these changes and then to have someone for whatever reason decide they don't like us because we are different.

Good grief! We are all different. And, that's okay. What is not okay is to have someone make fun of you or treat you badly because of that difference.

I'm really passionate about this subject! It not only happened to me, but bullying is happening to millions of kids in schools all over the United States. The school I attend, Carver Preparatory is no exception.

Looks like the God Squad has their work cut out for them. So, come along, join me and the other members of the God Squad in this episode of the Giant Slayers.

Chapter 1

The locker corridor-usually teeming with the crush of loud boisterous students and clanging locker doors-was now eerily silent as she approached. Her footsteps echoed loudly throughout the dimly lit corridor, as she cautiously entered. Casting a wary glance about, she hesitated listening, then tentatively continued all the while looking around assuring herself no one was in sight.

Quickly, she made her way to locker-128B-located halfway down the corridor. She exhaled loudly, allowing her breath to escape in a loud whooshing sound that echoed ominously through the empty corridor startling her. Glancing from one end of the corridor to the other assuring herself, she was still alone, she hunched her shoulders and turned her attention to the lock. Her fingers trembled. Pulling on the lock, it did not open. She tried again. Again, the lock did not open. Tears of frustration formed in her eyes as she leaned her head against the locker. Closing her eyes and taking a deep breath, she wiped her sweaty palms on her skirt, steadied herself and tried again. Breathe, she said, taking a shaky breath; just breathe.

The sound of footsteps echoing through the corridor followed closely by the voices of two girls entering the corridor startled her. Tensing her body, she turned quickly to face the oncoming girls, her back pressed tightly against the locker. As they approached, her heart thumped wildly in her chest. Warily, she watched as they came closer.

"Hey, Taylor," one of the girls greeted. Not waiting for a reply, she and her companion continued down the corridor, stopping a few feet away. The girl that greeted Taylor stepped forward, opened her locker and retrieved what she needed all the while talking to her friend.

Satisfied they were not interested in her, Taylor, turned back to the locker. Her breath escaped with a loud sigh. Get a grip, she sternly scolded herself pressing her hand against her pounding chest. You're being silly. Now concentrate. Her eyes fell on the locker number something was not right. The numbering was different. Upon closer inspection the numbering looked as if it had been altered. If she had not been so nervous, she would have noticed right away. She looked to the locker to the right of where she stood—125B. So, this had to be 126B. Someone had changed the numbers. She moved down to the left, finding another 128B. Dialing her combination, she pulled on the lock. The lock opened.

That's strange she thought, as she retrieved the books she needed. I really must be letting those girls get to me. They have me so scattered, I don't even know my own locker. Shrugging her shoulders, she dismissed her thoughts, intent upon getting the right book for tonight's homework and getting out of the corridor as quickly as possible.

"Well look who's here," the familiar voice behind her announced.

A feeling of dread washed over Taylor. Her mind began casting about trying to figure out where had they come from? Why did she not hear them? Her hand trembled slightly as slowly, she closed her locker and set the lock all the time thinking what she should do. Taking a shaky breath, and purposefully setting her face, Taylor turned only inches from the one person she had so desperately been trying to avoid—Marcie. And, Marcie wasn't alone.

This came as no surprise to Taylor. She knew because only a few months before she had been a part of Marcie's inner circle.

As she looked from Marcie to the girls standing on either side of her she thought of the times she had spent with Marcie. Joining her for lunch and spending hours talking about hair, clothes and boys. And, as uncomfortable as it made her, she also had been one of those that had joined Marcie in doing this very thing to some other girl. Frowning, she faced Marcie and braced herself for what was to come.

"Hey, Marcie," Taylor spoke clutching the large biology book to her chest, relieved her voice came out strong and clear although inwardly she was trembling. Cautiously, she eyed the girls standing around her. She could see the girl to the right of Marcie stood slightly back creating a space she could slip through if she could distract Marcie and move quickly enough.

"Marcie," she blurted loudly while at the same time pushing her way through the narrow space. Having successfully maneuvered herself through the space, putting a safe distance between her and the others, she turned momentarily to face Marcie; "I would love to stay and talk but I'm late." Willing herself not to run, Taylor quickly strode down the corridor not seeing the surprised look on the faces of the girls left standing looking after her.

"Hey Taylor," Marcie called; "that was rude. You didn't even say excuse me."

"Yeah," the other two echoed.

The last thing Taylor heard as she escaped the corridor was their laughter. As quickly as she could she put the corridor behind her.

A quick glance behind assured she was not being followed. She began to run. First a jog, then faster and faster. She ran blindly. Heart pounding. Tears spilling from her eyes, running down her face. She did not stop. She ran. She ran past other students. Off the campus. Not even the screeching of brakes, or the blaring horn of the irritated driver that shouted at her could stop her. She ran covering the five blocks to her home.

As she neared her house, she began to sob. Louder and louder. She ran up the front steps taking them two at a time. Bursting through the door, her sobs shattered the quietness as she blindly fled up the stairs and into her bedroom. She did not stop when her mother came out of the kitchen to see what all the commotion was about.

"Taylor, Taylor. What's going on? What's wrong?" her Mother questioned.

But Taylor did not stop. Entering the safety of her bedroom; slamming the door, she threw the book she had clutched in her hands to the floor, cast off her backpack, and flung herself face down on her bed. Burying her face into the soft pillows she screamed out her agony, the pillow muffling the sound. With each sob, her stomach convulsed causing her to curl her body into a tight ball.

Taylor wasn't aware her mother had entered the room. She felt her gather her into her arms and gently begin to rock her as she continued to wail like some hurt animal. How long she cried, she did not know. All she knew was here she was safe. Here, she didn't have to look over her shoulder to see if she was being followed. She didn't have to pretend the mean comments did not hurt her. Here in her room, in her mother's arms, holding her, rocking her, she felt safe. She didn't want to leave her mother's embrace or her room ever again.

"Mom," Taylor turned her tear-streaked face up to her mother, "please don't make me go back there. Please Mom! I can't take anymore," she wailed as her voice rose hysterically.

"Taylor," her mother soothed, "what are you talking about, go back where?"

"School," Taylor lamented, "I can't go back there! Mom, you must promise me you won't make me go back. I, I can't go back there. I, I, I'll kill myself! I would rather die than go back there. Please, don't make me go back."

"Shh, shh, baby," her mother soothed clutching her daughter tightly in her arms. "I don't want you saying anything about killing yourself or dying. It's going to be alright, you will see."

"No, no, Mom," Taylor wailed looking up at her Mom, her eyes pleading with her to understand. "It will never be alright. Those girls hate me, and they will always be there to make my life miserable."

"Honey, we'll go see the principal…"

"You don't understand," Taylor's voice rose in frustration, "the principal can't help. She can't stop them. No one can. They are just going to keep coming after me and coming after me!"

"Alright Taylor, alright," her mother soothed trying to ease her daughter's distress.

"Please, Mom, please, don't make me go back there!"

"Shh, Shh, baby," her mother cooed rocking her distraught daughter while stroking her hair. How long she sat holding Taylor she did not know. But she did know something had to be done to help Taylor and as her mother, she was the one that needed to act regardless of what Taylor said.

This was too much. Enough was enough. She had tried to be patient. Tried to let the principal, Ms. Mallard handle it. As far as she was concerned things had gone way past what Ms. Mallard termed *girls being girls!*

Mrs. Williams did not know exactly what had caused her daughter to run home crying, but she had a good idea it had something to do with that Marcie girl. Yes, something had to be done but for now Taylor needed comforting. She continued to rock and gently stroke Taylor's hair. Gradually Taylor's sobs subsided to an occasional shuddering intake of breath. Her even breathing, told Mrs. Williams, Taylor had fallen asleep.

Gently, she eased Taylor onto the bed and covered her with a lightweight, tattered pink throw, Taylor's favorite blanket since she was a toddler. Standing, she looked down at the red-splotched face of her daughter. She looked more like a five-year-old than a twelve-year-old, pre-teen.

Bending, she wiped Taylor's bangs away from her eyes— bangs that she had told Taylor were too long seeing she was always swiping them out of her eyes. A small unbidden smile tugged at the corner of her mouth at the memory. She ached for her daughter as she placed a kiss on Taylor's forehead then quietly left the room, her mind filled with many things.

As she searched through the pile of business cards stacked on her desk, she remembered Taylor from only a few months earlier. How eager she had been for the starting of a new semester. She was happy, surrounded by her BFF, Marcie and the other members of the group. Talking on the phone with them and sharing in long afternoon study sessions. Life seemed to be going well for Taylor.

Mrs. Williams remembered how she had been so pleased that Taylor appeared to be adjusting quite nicely to all the many changes and challenges of puberty. On more than one occasion, she had secretly felt sorry for the mothers that confided in her about the woes of their adolescent daughters. But all that had changed in what seemed like only a few days but in fact had been weeks. The dreaded adolescent behavior she had heard so much about from other parents of tween girls had now caught up with Taylor.

Mrs. Williams discovered she was not prepared for the unusual bursts of sass, the uncharacteristic displays of temper and the moodiness. Trying not to be overly concerned, she had comforted herself with the knowledge that this was only a phase and it too would pass. She assured herself that if she could survive the terrible two's, there was no way, she couldn't get through adolescence. But lately, she was finding it difficult to deal with the changes Taylor was experiencing.

Taylor had begun challenging her rules. At first it was being a few minutes late getting home from school which Taylor explained away with "Me and my friends were busy, and I lost track of time." But when Taylor started coming home late more and more, Mrs. Williams told her the "I lost track of time" was no longer acceptable.

After being on punishment for three days, Taylor got home on time. When she arrived, she would loudly stomp up the stairs, slam the door to her room, put her earphones on, and not emerge until time for dinner. That was one thing that hadn't changed about Taylor, she had a very healthy appetite. It was a good thing. Dinner time was the only time Mrs. Williams saw Taylor or had a chance to talk with her. Or, as was the case more and more attempt to talk with her.

In one of the rare times she had a conversation that was more than grunts, shoulder hunching, and head nodding; Taylor had talked about Marcie. It was Marcie this, and Marcie said that, and Marcie was the coolest girl at school. It troubled Mrs. Williams that Taylor was so taken with whatever Marcie said or did.

She knew she had reason to be concerned after she overheard Taylor talking with Marcie on the phone about one of her classmates. Mrs. Williams sat Taylor down for a stern lecture. Even though Taylor had appeared remorseful and assured her Mom it was harmless. "All the kids do it." Mrs. Williams' concerns were not put to rest and she began to pay closer attention to Taylor's interaction with Marcie.

To Taylor's horror, Mrs. Williams started volunteering for activities at school she knew the girls would be attending. Once while serving as a chaperone for a school dance, Mrs. Williams noticed that Marcie, Taylor, and three other girls separated themselves from everyone else. The girls appeared to be popular as they greeted and briefly interacted with the other students, but they stayed within their small group.

Mrs. Williams could not quite put her finger on why this bothered her. Maybe, it was because after the girls had greeted someone, they turned to each other, whispered back and forth, and burst into laughter, while watching the other person. Maybe it was Taylor's snooty manner when meeting up with other girls from her class when she was out shopping or running errands with her. Mrs. Williams realized it was many things.

She tried talking to Taylor telling her:

"What kind of friend is Marcie to you? If she will talk about another girl to you, believe me she will talk about you to others."

Taylor had just laughed, rolled her eyes and with a wave of her hand and all the confidence of a twelve-year-old dismissed her mother's warning, proclaiming:

"Marcie and I are the best of friends, we're like this," she said holding up her two fingers and crossing them. "She would n-e-v-e-r talk about me behind my back. Just like I would n-e-v-e-r talk about her behind her back. Stop worrying Mom, I can handle this!"

Shaking her head at the memory, Mrs. Williams continued searching through her desk. If only that had been true. Just as she had warned Taylor, the tables turned. When it first began, Mrs. Williams had insisted she and Taylor meet with Principal Mallard. The principal had assured her she would take care of the situation right away. Said it sounded like a case of *girls being girls*.

While Principal Mallard handled the situation, Taylor became more withdrawn. She made up excuses not to go to school. When she did go, she returned home and went straight to her room. Even her appetite was being affected. Her grades were falling and out of desperation, Mrs. Williams had sought the advice of her pastor.

Her pastor recommended a counselor he said had done wonders with other girls. Said if she wasn't too busy, maybe she could see Taylor.

Mrs. Williams had not readily acted on the advice of her pastor as things had seemingly returned to normal between Taylor and Marcie, or so she thought until today. Taylor coming home in hysterics and talking about wanting to die if she had to return to school had alarmed Mrs. Williams.

This *girls being girls* thing had gone on long enough. Taylor was not able to handle this. Finding what she was looking for, Mrs. Williams dialed the number on the card her pastor had given her.

"Hello, Ms. Foster…"

Chapter 2

The sun beamed brightly through the sheer curtained window signaling the beginning of a new day. Angel woke from her troubled sleep. Pulling the covers over her head and turning her back to the intruding sunlight, she groaned loudly trying to ignore the incessant voice of her mother at her bedroom door.

"Angelica!" her mother called. "Get up! You're going to be late. I need you to walk Amber to school this morning."

"I'm no baby Mom," Amber spoke up close behind her mother. "I don't need her to walk me to school. I can walk with my friends."

"Hush Amber," her mother reprimanded. "You are only eight and I won't have you walking to school by yourself. Now, Angelica get up! I've got to leave shortly."

"Okay, okay," Angel replied groggily. "I'm getting up... see," she said swinging her legs out of the bed. Stretching Angel stood, yawned loudly and headed for the bathroom across the hall. As she splashed cold water on her face, she could hear her sister trying to convince their mother she didn't need Angel to walk her to school as they walked down the stairs.

A short time later Angel entered the kitchen feeling more awake. Her hair, which the steam from the shower caused to poof out, still framed her face and cascaded down her back in a mass of unruly curls.

The remnants of the dream evaporated as she slipped into the chair at the table next to her younger sister. Grabbing a piece of toast, she began slathering it with butter.

"Wow, Angel," Amber announced. "Look at your hair!"

"What's wrong with it?" Angel questioned giving her sister a hard look.

"It's way out there," Amber answered spreading her arms apart.

"So, what?" It's my hair so don't worry about it."

"I was just saying…"

"Amber, Angel, both of you stop that bickering right now.

"But, Mom…"

"Amber, did you hear me tell you to stop?"

"Yes Ma'am" Amber replied giving Angel a sideways glance. Angel didn't see the look as she was busy stuffing a piece of buttered toast into her mouth.

"Doesn't look like that bad dream you had made you lose your appetite," Amber announced.

"Shhhh," Angel hissed sending a warning look to her sister quickly glancing back at her Mom hoping she was too occupied to hear Amber's comment.

"What's this about a bad dream?" her mother asked coming to the table and depositing a bowl of hot grits in front of Angel dispelling any hope that she had not overheard Amber's remark. Returning to the stove Angel watched as her mother cracked a lone egg into the hot skillet letting it cook just until the yolk was starting to harden, and the white was slightly crispy around the edges, just the way Angel liked. Flipping the egg, she let it cook a little longer, then returned to the table, depositing the egg on top of Angel's bowl of grits.

Angel mixed the egg into the grits then sprinkled salt and pepper on top. One more stir to make sure everything was mixed together just right. Perfect, she thought spooning the mixed concoction into her mouth before speaking.

"Nothing, Mom, really," Angel answered between mouthfuls. "Guess it was that root beer float I had with the girls."

"Yeah," Amber interjected unable to contain her knowledge of Angel's restless night; "that's why you were crying and telling someone to leave you alone?"

"Why don't you just be quiet?" Angel spoke harshly to Amber. "So, I had a bad dream or whatever, why are you making a big deal of it? It's none of your business anyway, so why don't you just shut-up!"

Amber's eyes widened in shock, her voice raised, she turned to her mother.

"Owww, Mom, Angel used the S word!"

"Angelica," her mother spoke sharply. "Don't talk to your sister like that. And, you know, we don't use that word."

"Yes ma'am," Angel replied tossing a glaring look Amber's way. Amber just smiled and wagged her head in satisfaction.

"What's this about a bad dream?" her mother asked coming to the table after placing the skillet into the sink to soak. "Something going on with you that we need to talk about?"

Angel looked into her mother's deep brown eyes. She looked tired, even after a night's sleep. She knew her mother had a lot on her these days. Recently, she had started working extra hours at the laundry to help with the household expenses. Things had been tough for them since their father had been laid off his job as a carpenter with a small construction company.

Angel had heard her parents talking late into the night. She could not make out their words, but she knew what they talked about was serious. In the past, their late-night conversations had been punctuated with laughter. Last night, there had been no laughter. Although muted, she had heard her father's voice raised in anger. A short time later, the door closed as he left for his late- night security job at a local factory. In the quietness of the night, she heard her mother crying.

No, Angel decided, she could not bring herself to tell her mother that she had had another one of *those* dreams as she called them. So instead, she put a smile on her face and as normally as she could answered.

"No worries, I'm good Mom. It was probably the float I had with the girls."

Angel's mother's eyes searched Angel's face intently. Sighing, she said; "Okay, if you're sure. But, when I get home tonight, we are going to talk."

"Okay," Angel shrugged giving her full attention to the last heap of grits in her bowl.

Checking her watch, Angel's mom jumped up, retrieved her house keys from the counter and her purse from the chair. "I've got to go! I don't want to miss my bus."

Bending she kissed Angel on the cheek and then Amber. Issuing Amber, a warning to obey her big sister, she hurried out the door.

"Angel, Angel..." Amber's voice broke through her thoughts. "Don't you hear me talking to you? What's with you?"

"Nothing. What do you want?"

"We gotta go or I'm going to be late. I promised my friends I would meet them at the corner at 8:00a.m and it's... 5... 10... 15 minutes and 5 seconds until eight."

Angel couldn't suppress the smile that came to her face. Her Mom had bought Amber the relatively inexpensive watch for her birthday which she was constantly referring to and telling anyone that would listen the time.

"We've got plenty of time," Angel replied taking her bowl to the sink and rinsing it. "Get your stuff. I'm ready."

"What about your hair?" Amber asked. "What about it?"

"Aren't you going to do something with it?"

"I thought I'd leave it like this since you're in such a hurry."

Checking her watch, Amber replied: "I am, but I can wait."

It had taken Angel only a few minutes to pull her hair into a high pony and twist it into a bun, which she secured with hair pins. Satisfied, that her hair would stay in place, she rushed down the stairs, locked the back door and walked Amber to school.

Leaving Amber and her friends at the entrance to Franklin Elementary, Angel made her way to the bus stop. She had to hurry if she wanted to meet up with the girls. Taking her seat on the bus, she allowed her mind to return to yesterday's meeting. How could she possibly help someone when she hadn't been able to help herself when she encountered the same issue? Perhaps she could talk to Ms. Foster when the others weren't around and convince her to give the lead to Chris. Chris would be the better choice.

As a peer mentor, Angel knew sometimes it could be challenging but until yesterday, she was confident in her ability to handle any situation that came her way. This assignment was different. She felt it the moment Ms. Foster showed the picture of the girl with the large doe–like, brown eyes. Something about the sadness that echoed from the depths of those eyes reached deep within Angel and touched a spot of vulnerability. Twice she had turned her head from the image of the girl uncomfortable with the feelings that rose up within her.

Cringing inwardly, Angel was reminded of that same helpless look from another twelve-year-old girl. Her thoughts disturbed her, and she shifted uncomfortably in her seat staring out the bus window. Her mind returning to the meeting. It had been difficult for her to pay attention to the images on the screen and listen to Ms. Foster's voice as she explained each image.

Angel could not suppress the heavy sigh of relief that escaped her lips when the screen faded to black and the lights were turned on. The heaviness that had set in at seeing the girl, shoulders slumped, sitting alone, staring into space seemed seared into her memory. She held her breath, let it out slowly, willing herself not to cry. She dared not look at the others sitting around the table lest a look break her resolve.

Ms. Foster's voice broke the heavy silence.

"Well, God Squad, are you willing to take on this assignment?"

The girls looked from one to the other. No one spoke. Angel could feel their eyes on her, but she kept her head down. Finally, Eve spoke.

"Ms. Foster, do you think we can help this girl? I mean what can we do? We're just students ourselves."

"Yeah," Jade joined in, "seems to me what is happening should be handled by the principal or some adult."

"I hear what you are saying," Ms. Foster responded, "but, at this time the principal does not view these instances as anything but *girls being girls*. She has met with all involved and seems that what is happening has been brewing for some time now. According to the principal, Ms. Mallard, the young lady—Taylor, the one you saw on the screen is not totally without fault in this matter. At this time, the principal is not willing to get involved; and her advice to the parents is to wait and see.

Should the girls not be able to work it out themselves, she will act. Ms. Mallard has assured the parents that letting the girls work it out amongst themselves is the best solution. She is confident that by the end of the semester they would be back to being the best of friends.

"So," Chris inquired, looking to Ms. Foster all the while lightly tapping her pencil on the notebook before her; "since its just *girls being girls*, why are you asking us to get involved?"

"That's a good question," Ms. Foster responded. "Normally, I would let it go but I've met with Taylor and her mother as well as the other students involved. And, I've done my own research, so to speak. After talking with the principal, the girls involved, and Taylor's mother, I don't believe this to be a case of *girls being girls*. No, quite the contrary. The pictures tell another story. Taylor is being affected by something or someone. What or whom, she will not say. But according to her mother, things are getting so bad with Taylor that she is seriously considering taking Taylor out of Carver Preparatory and transferring her to Market Academy."

"Market Academy," Jade exclaimed … "is way across town. It'll take a full hour to get there by bus."

"You're right Jade," Mia interjected, "she will have to get up at 5:00 o'clock in the morning to get to school on time."

"Yeah," Jade said. "Poor kid won't be doing anything but riding buses."

"What does riding a bus have to do with anything?" Angel broke in noticeably upset. Giving Mia and Jade a hard look, she continued. "I think what's important here is getting …what's her name…some help right away."

"Her name is Taylor," Ms. Foster supplied.

"Okay, I Angel, think we, the God Squad," Angel indicated the girls assembled around the table, "need to be the ones to help Taylor."

"Gosh Angel," Jade replied, "I didn't mean to upset you. I was concerned about Taylor having to transfer way across town and…"

"I know," Angel interrupted cutting off any further explanation. "I will say it again; the bus ride is not what is important here!"

"Angel, Jade," Ms. Foster broke in. "This is a discussion. All ideas and opinions are welcomed. We are not fighting against one another. And, in any discussion, we are to what…?" she asked directing the question to Angel.

"Respect the other person," Angel mumbled shifting uncomfortably in her chair. Folding her arms across her chest, she focused her eyes downward refusing to look up.

"I'm sorry Angel," Ms. Foster said. "I didn't hear you and I'm sure the others didn't either."

Angel looked up fixing Jade with a hard stare, her voice coming out louder than she intended "I said respect the other person."

"Angel," Ms. Foster corrected Angel. "Do you think you are being respectful to Jade and the others in the group? You appear to be upset. I am wondering if we should stop talking about Taylor and focus our attention on you. Based upon your attitude, it appears there is something else going on? Would you like to talk about it?"

Angel turned her angry glance to Ms. Foster. With arms still folded across her chest, she opened her mouth to speak, the torrent of words forming a lump in her throat. Angel felt she would burst into tears if she said anything. Quickly she lowered her eyes, shook her head and hunched her shoulders dismissing the invitation.

Ms. Fosters' gaze rested on Angel even though Angel was now obviously avoiding eye contact with her. Trying once again she invited Angel to speak.

"Are you sure you don't want to talk?"

Angel raised her head willing herself to hold Ms. Foster's gaze. Before answering she stiffened her back, sitting up straight in her chair, folding her hands on the table before her. In her most controlled voice, she replied.

"No, I don't want to talk."

Ms. Foster's gaze lingered on Angel for a few moments longer. Only the slight raising of her right eyebrow indicated she was not quite convinced with Angel's attempt to show her everything was alright. When Angel did not respond, she did not press her.

"Alright, girls, let's continue."

Now that it was safe to talk, Sadie's soft voice broke the awkward silence.

"I agree with Angel. Taylor is here at Carver Prep and we are "peer mentors" she emphasized. We've been talking about this kind of thing since before summer break when Eve and Chris helped Kelsey with those girls that were bullying her. As peer mentors we could be a very big help to Taylor, her parents, and the student body for that matter."

"I'm with Angel and Sadie," Eve spoke. "Going to another school doesn't seem to be the best solution. Especially, well, the same thing might happen at Market Academy."

"And, more than likely will" Chris interjected. "I've been doing some research on this subject for one of my classes. What I've learned is that girls our age and younger are very likely to be bullied especially, if you are new in school or different in some way. So, I agree with Angel and Sadie. It is time Carver Preparatory face it; we have a bullying problem. Come on guys, Chris asked, eyes going from one girl to the next. "You cannot have forgotten how it was when you first came here? If I'm not mistaken, each of us was the target of bullying."

"Well, yeah," Mia said, briefly recalling her own encounter with bullies. "I remember how it was but, it didn't affect me like it is affecting Taylor."

"Maybe not, Mia, but you must admit, it did affect you."

"Yeah, I was kind of freaked out for a minute. But then I met you, Eve and Angel," Mia replied her voice trailing off.

"That's my point," Chris emphasized. "You met us, the God Squad. Well, we weren't the God Squad then, but the point is, you met us. And as Sadie said, Kelsey met us. Taylor needs to meet us, the God Squad!"

"Now we are getting somewhere," Ms. Foster said. "Does this mean you are willing to accept this assignment?"

The girls looked from one to the other than back at Ms. Foster.

"I'm in," Mia spoke casting a guarded look in Angel's direction.

"I already said I'm in," Chris added. "With the research I'm doing, I would be interested in taking the lead on this assignment."

Silence followed. All eyes rested on Jade.

"What?" Jade asked in exasperation.

"You know," Chris responded; "are you for the assignment or not?"

"I never said I wasn't for it," Jade defended. "I just mentioned that it would be a long bus ride to Market Academy."

"Oh, Jade," Sadie replied. "Can't you let that go?"

"No," Jade said. "I think having to ride the bus is important and you're all taking Angel's side saying that what I think is not important."

"We're not saying that what you think is not important," Chris explained looking to the others for agreement. The others except for Angel nodded their heads.

"It's that we're focusing more on helping Taylor and not so much about her having to ride the bus."

"Jade, I'm sorry," Angel apologized. "What you said about Taylor having to ride the bus is very important; it's, she drew in a shaky breath before continuing. It's, this whole bullying situation hits close to home and I'm not handling it very well. Would you forgive me?"

Jade, eyes widened in amazement unable to believe what she was hearing and seeing. Angel apologizing and looking like she was about to cry? Angel definitely wasn't being her typical self. Whatever had happened in the past must have been tough.

"Sure Angel, I forgive you," Jade said. "But, don't get mad at me; maybe you will feel a lot better if you talk about what's bothering you?"

Angel pondered Jade's words before answering;

"I will… but right now, I'm not ready to talk about it. Is that okay with all of you?" She looked from one girl to the next. With a nod of the head each girl assured Angel it was okay.

"Will you be alright?" Ms. Foster asked her voice full of concern. "Seems like this assignment is bringing up some unresolved issues for you?"

Angel hesitated, drew in a deep breath before answering, "You're right, it has brought up some things I haven't talked about. But, I promise, I will talk about them later."

"Alright Angel" Ms. Foster said, "We will respect your wishes. In the meantime, she continued focusing her eyes on each of the other girls and drawing their attention from Angel, "we are in agreement our next mission is Taylor Williams?"

"Yes!" they yelled in unison.

"Good," Ms. Foster's smile included each one. "Let's get to work. We have a lot to cover before you meet with Taylor. And, Chris, I know you would do an excellent job taking the lead on this assignment but, I want Angel to be the lead.

Chapter 3

Angel sat through the rest of the meeting only hearing bits and pieces of what Ms. Foster was explaining. She knew it was important as twice Ms. Foster had stopped to ask if she was paying attention. Twice, she looked up from her blank notepad to catch either one or the other girls looking at her or the concerned look of Ms. Foster. Each time she battled the emotions that threatened to spill out and resisted the urge to get up and run from the room.

When her emotions threatened to get the best of her and she felt she could take it no more, Ms. Foster had ended the meeting, asking Chris to lead them in prayer. All through the prayer, Angel shifted her weight from one foot to the other, the petition for peace and strength mere words that in no way penetrated the emotional upheaval she was trying to hold in check. Her only thought was to get out and away from there as soon as possible.

Before Chris could finish saying amen, Angel broke from the group, grabbed up her things and hurried away ignoring any attempts by the others to talk with her or their concerned looks that followed as she bolted from the sanctuary.

Intentionally avoiding the first bus stop knowing the girls would be there soon, Angel quickly walked past it to the next a couple of blocks away. She needed to get her emotions in check before she felt she could talk to anyone, especially the girls. No matter how fast she walked, she could not stop the thoughts and images that filled her mind. She chided herself for acting so childish.

"How silly can you be," she thought; "running away from the sanctuary like some baby. You're almost sixteen for goodness sakes. What is wrong with you?"

But the image of the girl with hauntingly sad eyes catapulted Angel back four years to a time when a small twelve- year-old girl had also suffered the taunts and jeers of her fellow students.

Breaking into a run as though to out distance her thoughts, she felt the hot tears pouring down her cheeks. A cramp in her side caused her to pause and seek the comfort of a park bench set back in a grassy, tree shaded area. Taking the bench, Angel mopped at the tears coursing down her cheeks, eyes turned inward seeing the helpless and lone figure of a petite girl with a mass of dark unruly curly hair crouched against a wall, head buried in arms wrapped around her small body as though to shield her from the taunting laughter of the group of girls surrounding her. They seemed like giants towering over her as she looked up pleading with them. The painful memories hurt more than the stitch in her side, and she wrapped her arms around her abdomen in a gesture of comfort as the memories now released rushed forward.

"Why don't you leave me alone," the little girl wailed tears coursing down her cheeks. Her pleas only seemed to add to the delight of the girls standing around her.

"Oh, look at the barbed wire-haired monkey, one of the girls taunted. She wants us to "leave her alone," she mimicked in a whiney voice.

"Hey, barbed wire-haired monkey," another girl taunted; "where did you get that hair?" she asked as she pushed her hand across the thick curly locks.

"S-t-o-p!" the little girl wailed flaying helplessly at the hand tangled in her thick curls. "Leave my hair alone."

"Oh, oh, my hand is stuck," the girl said in exaggeration, pulling viciously on the tangled mass. Releasing her hand, she shrieked, "Ewww, my hands all greasy! Quick, somebody give me a hand sanitizer. I don't want to get cooties!

The group of girls laughed as if what was said was the funniest thing they had ever heard while the little girl smarting from the tearing away of her hair cried quietly keeping her head buried in her arms. She wanted to fight but knew that would only make things worse. Maybe, if she just endured their taunting, they would go away and leave her alone.

"Hey, monkey," the leader of the group continued, "what you got to say about that?" When no response was forthcoming, she sighed deeply, a satisfied smile pulling at the corners of her lips. "I'm bored," she announced stifling an imaginary yawn. "Old barbed wire-haired monkey here ain't no fun. Not only is she a wire-haired monkey, she's a chicken."

"Yeah," the other girls chimed in, "she's nothing but a chicken! Cluck, cluck, cluck."

Taking the little girl by the hair, the leader of the group tugged on it until the girl lifted her head. She leaned down bringing her face so close the little girl could feel the breath of her words, "Let this be a warning to you. You might think you are cute and all that, but believe me, you are the only one that thinks so. And, in case you didn't know, this is my school and I'm the Queen Bee around here. You understand?"

All the little girl could do was nod her head.

"Oh, and as for Stephen Banks, understand, he is MY boyfriend. There is no way he would like a shrimpy, barbed wire-haired monkey like you when he has me. So, stay away from him or I will make your life a living hell. Do you hear me?" She emphasized her words by tugging on the little girl's hair.

"Are you alright?" a gentle voice asked causing Angel to jump at the unexpected interruption. Bringing her eyes into focus she realized an older woman had come and sat on the bench beside her. The woman carried a large shopping bag and a black purse.

Why Angel focused on the shopping bag and purse she did not know.

"Are you alright?" the gentle voice inquired again.

Angel looked up into the bluest eyes she had ever seen, their color intensified by the dark bronze tone of the woman's skin. They sparkled and glowed seeming to emit a brilliance that immediately captured Angel's attention. As she stared into their depths, she felt herself becoming calmer.

"I'm alright," she stammered swiping at the tears on her cheeks. "Just got a cramp in my side and sat here until it passed."

"You probably need to drink some water," the older woman supplied reaching into the large bag and pulling out a small bottle of water; "and you might want to blow your nose," she continued pulling a handkerchief from her bag. "Here, my dear," she offered handing first the handkerchief and then the bottle of water to Angel.

Angel took the hankie, blew her nose. Looking from the hankie to the woman, "I don't think you want this back?" she said.

"No, child" the older woman replied with a chuckle. "You may keep it. I have plenty more of those."

Angel tucked the hankie away in her backpack. Taking the water, she opened it and took a small sip from the bottle.

"Oh, no" the older lady said, "drink some more. It's hot out and you probably been running quite a distance at least from the looks of you, you been running some distance, so you need more than that little sip."

Angel took a long swallow of the water. As much as she hated to admit it, she felt better. Calmer, she felt the gentle breeze upon her face, cooling her hot cheeks.

"Now, don't you feel better?" the older woman asked seeing the redness recede from Angel's face. "Sometimes, all it takes is a little water... and a gentle breeze to make everything alright again." As if on cue, a light breeze flowed past cooling Angel's face and fluttering her hair.

"I guess so, Angel replied. "Thank you for the water."

"No trouble little one, no trouble at all," the older woman assured her openly staring at her. Angel found herself uncomfortable under the woman's unwavering look.

"By the way," the older woman asked, "has anyone ever told you, you are beautiful and... you have the most wonderful curly hair!"

Angel's hand went automatically to press down her unruly curls at the mention of her hair. No one had ever called her hair wonderful. The seemingly sincere compliment brought a lump into Angel's throat keeping her from speaking. All she could do was to shake her head no and stare into those mesmerizing blue eyes.

"Well you are, beautiful that is, and you do have the most wonderful hair!" the older woman continued smiling warmly at Angel. "May I," she asked reaching out to touch Angel's hair. Angel nodded. Picking up a lock of Angel's hair she held it in her hand. "So silky and soft," she continued. "Such wonderful hair! I bet you get compliments all the time about your hair."

Her eyes gently looked over Angel's face as she took Angel's hand into her warm grasp. "Yes, my dear. You are truly a work of art, a masterpiece. God didn't make junk when He made you," she said allowing her warm blue gaze to look directly into Angel's eyes. "You are quite beautiful. And, don't you believe anyone that tells you differently. You hear me?"

Angel sat immobilized, entranced by the woman's eyes and her soothing voice. At her question she simply nodded her head and in a small voice answered, "Yes ma'am."

"Good," the older woman said, a gentle smile spreading across her face causing the lines around her eyes to come into view and the blue of her eyes to sparkle. Patting Angel's hand, she sighed... "Well, Angel, I best be on my way." Rising slowly from the bench, adjusting her large shopping bag and black purse, the older woman turned walking away.

Angel sat unable to move watching the woman as she started down the sidewalk. Taking a few steps, the older woman stopped and turned back to face Angel.

"Remember," she said raising her finger upward and briefly winking, "don't forget, God didn't make junk when He made you."

"I won't," Angel replied, her hand going to her hair and a small smile curving the corners of her mouth. "I won't forget."

Giving an approving nod and a smile at Angel's answer, the older woman walked away.

"Hey, Angel," Mia's familiar voice called. Angel turned to see the girls rushing toward her. Standing, she waited for them to reach her.

"Wait up!" Mia yelled. A broad grin spread across Angel's face as she watched the girls make their way to her.

"Girl, we been trying to catch you ever since you left the sanctuary," Mia spoke between swallowing gulps of air.

"Yeah, you know it is going to take more than you getting angry to keep us away," Jade interjected breathless from running.

"Got that right," Eve said, "We are in this together."

"Yeah," Sadie added, "you know if there is something wrong with one of us, the rest of us are out of sorts until things are right again."

Chris moved in close to Angel, "Come on girl," she said, wrapping her arm across Angel's shoulder and the other around Jade's shoulder, "group hug, it'll make you feel better."

The other girls entwined their arms forming a tight circle. Angel threw back her head shaking her hair, setting her mane of riotous curls free with the movement. Laughter flowed up from deep within her being, filling the air around her with its happy sound. Startled birds perched in a nearby tree fluttered into the air.

"Thanks guys," she said, sandwiched tightly between Chris and Jade. "I'm sure glad you showed up. I do feel better, but that older woman down there had already made me feel better."

"What woman?" Eve asked.

"The older woman walking down the street," Angel answered turning to show Eve.

They all turned in the direction Angel indicated. "Well, there was a woman," Angel replied, her voice trailing off, a confused look on her face as she searched the empty sidewalk.

"Come on," Chris teased, "let's get this girl a cold drink. She must be having a heat stroke or something. Seeing old ladies and stuff!"

"Yeah," Sadie replied good-naturedly, "next thing you know, she will be telling us she saw an angel."

Angel stopped, turned and looked once more in the direction the older woman had taken. A quizzical look on her face with the beginning of a question in her mind… Shrugging her shoulders, she smiled remembering those wonderful blue eyes! With a toss of her curly hair, the words of the woman echoing in her mind— God don't make junk—Angel fell in step with the girls as they made their way across the street toward the diner and the best root beer floats in the world!

Chapter 4

The beginnings of another idyllic fall day had begun. The birds chirped gaily from the branches of the large maple tree growing close to Taylor's window. Its leaves were beginning to take on the vibrant reds and oranges of fall, Taylor's favorite time of the year.

She loved fall! The colors and the colder weather that allowed her to wear bulky sweaters and short wool plaid skirts with stockings and boots! But lately, she had not been as enchanted with this time of year.

The smell of bacon frying wafted up the stairs tickling her nose as she lay asleep in her large double bed. Pulling the pink coverlet over her head, she fought against the enticing smell that pulled her from sleep.

Throwing the cover from her head and flopping onto her back she starred blindly at the ceiling. Her stomach growled prompting her to sit up. Her eyes took in the beauty of the room she called Taylor's Den.

A romantic by nature, Taylor had decorated her room in the style known as Shabby Chic filling it with lace and floral-patterned fabrics in varying shades of pink with white lace accents. Old-fashioned frames with intricate scrolling held her fondest pictures from childhood. A white painted dressing table with a hand stenciled round mirror and a floral printed skirt had been an old, in need of repair, table salvaged from a discard pile and dragged home by her. With the help of her mother it had been turned into a wonderful dressing table that she loved. The chair another salvaged piece was painted white with the cushion covered in bright pink velvet.

Her eyes traveled across the room to the window seat decorated with pink velvet and gingham checked fabric pillows. She had loved sitting there feeling the sun on her face or as the weather grew colder wrapping up in her favorite pink blanket, reading, daydreaming or writing in her journal, sharing her secrets with the old maple tree.

A small desk held Taylor's computer and a small, light pink lamp covered with a sheer pink beaded scarf served as a desk lamp. On it, her second most favorite possession, a bright pink mouse pad with the words Taylor's Den in large black Edwardian Script given as a gift from her mother two years ago. Now the letters were faded and the pink not as bright as was her joy in the gift.

These days, she rarely sat at the desk except to do an occasional homework assignment. When questioned by her mother why she wasn't using her computer, she had said she was doing her homework on the school's computers. She did not want to tell her mother that she was getting mean messages in her email from people she did not know.

Pulling her knees up to her chest, she laid her chin on her knees looking around her room. Once she had taken joy in her handiwork and sharing her latest creation with her best friend Marcie. She and Marcie were inseparable since meeting in grammar school. Each day was new and exciting, and she eagerly looked forward to each new day bouncing out of bed with a smile on her face and a song on her lips.

She was outgoing, liked by many and envied by even more. She enjoyed school and her classes, especially her art class. And, the best part of it all, she and Marcie were part of the most elite group of girls in the entire school! A group in which she and Marcie were the center.

But that had changed. No longer was Taylor part of Marcie's inner circle, she had been cast out and become the object of Marcie's ridicule, vicious gossip, and hurtful pranks.

No longer one of Marcie's chosen ones, she had been forced to find new friends. At first, she was reluctant to mingle with others but two of the girls in her art class befriended her and went out of their way to include her in their activities. She found herself enjoying their company and before long the three of them along with another girl had joined together becoming another one of the "groups" that congregated around the Quad before the start of classes each day.

Taylor was starting to enjoy her new group of friends oblivious to the subtle attack began by Marcie. At first it was just a burst of giggles, cold stares, and ignored greetings as she and her group walked by. Lately, the giggles included comments like, "Do you believe she wore that; or look at her hair," followed by more giggles.

And it did not stop there. A lone email from one of the girls in Marcie's circle showed up. Hoping the email was an apology or even an acceptance back into the group, Taylor had eagerly opened it only to find a message that left no doubt she wasn't wanted in the group. But that was not the only email she received. Numerous others followed. Some accused her of being a traitor. Some called her a pig, others a slut. She didn't even know what slut meant but she knew it couldn't be good. One day after several particularly vicious emails, she shut her computer off and hadn't turned it on since.

And, with the incidence in the locker corridor, even Taylor's beautiful room with its many handmade items could not dispel the dark cloud that engulfed her.

Curling her body in a tight knot, Taylor turned on her side, pulling the cover over her head, debating whether she would go to school or not.

She could always use her sure-fire excuse-cramps. No sooner had the thought entered her mind then she quickly discarded it remembering her mother's threat of taking her to the doctor. Groaning and flopping onto her back, she reasoned that being subject to an examination by the doctor made school seem pleasant in comparison. A knock at her door brought all thoughts to a halt.

"Taylor are you up?" her mother questioned coming into the room. Seeing Taylor still in bed she admonished her, "You don't want to be late. And, if you don't get up now you will miss breakfast."

"I'm getting up now," Taylor replied the irritation sounding in her voice. "If you just go, I'll get ready and be down stairs shortly."

Mrs. Williams ignored her daughter's irritation.

Okay, I'll expect you in twenty minutes, she replied. "If you're not down stairs by then I'm taking you to the doctor."

"Okay, okay," Taylor grumbled her reply as she made her way to the bathroom oblivious of the concern that etched her mother's face.

After Taylor gulped down a glass of milk and squashed her bacon and scrambled eggs between two slices of buttered toast, she joined her mother in the car. Taking a large bite of her make shift breakfast sandwich, Taylor ignored her mother as they made their way to the school.

"Taylor," her mother said, "slow down, take smaller bites. That sandwich isn't going anywhere."

Taylor stuffed the last bite of her sandwich into her mouth just as they pulled up to the front of the school.

"Will you be alright?" Mrs. Williams asked as she pulled up to the school.

Swallowing loudly and licking her fingers before answering, Taylor replied:

"I'll be fine, if you're concerned that I'm going to come running home crying like I did the other day, I'm not. I can handle Marcie and her group. So, stop worrying."

"Well, yes, but…"

"But what? There is no but, Mom. We are staying away from each other and everything is fine. So just let it go, will you? Anyway, that counselor…Ms. Foster, has scheduled me to meet with a peer mentor, so I'll be fine." She did not bother to tell her mother, she had no intention of meeting with a peer mentor.

"I hope so," Mrs. Williams sighed deciding not to say what was on her mind.

"You don't have to worry Mom. It's no big deal. Remember, it's just *girls being girls*." Taylor threw over her shoulder as she stepped out of the car.

"Okay, I'll pick you up after school."

"That won't be necessary Mom, I'm going to walk home with my friends."

"Taylor…," Mrs. Williams began. Seeing the defiant look on Taylor's face, she thought better of her next words. Discarding them she said, "I love you honey. Have a good day."

Taylor raised an eyebrow, smiled turned and walked away. As soon as she entered the building she cast about a wary glance. Being back in school with the possibility of another confrontation with Marcie and her group left Taylor feeling anything but confident. The thought of running into Marcie and her group set her teeth on edge and unconsciously she clenched her jaw.

Checking outside, she quickly made her way down the corridor to the back exit and out into the main Quad where students gathered before classes. Stopping momentarily, Taylor scanned the groups spotting her friends; zig zagging her way across the concrete expanse she made her way to where they were gathered. Sighing, relieved, she joined her group entering the conversation all the while keeping an eye out for Marcie.

"Hey Taylor," her friends greeted.

"Girl you missed it yesterday," Amy confided drawing closer to Taylor. "Marcie and her group really made a scene in the cafeteria at lunch."

"Yeah but tell her what happened before the cafeteria in-ci-dent," Rebecca reminded Amy.

"Oh, yeah, I almost forgot about that," Amy said. "Well, before that me and Sarah were in the restroom and Marcie and her group came in and started talking trash about Sarah. They tried to start something then, but we just ignored them and walked out. Anyway, when we went to the cafeteria for lunch, one of Marcie's girls waited until Sarah had gotten her tray and would you believe," pausing for emphasis, "she bumped into Sarah."

"So," Taylor responded.

"So…" Rebecca interjected, eyes wide, "corn and gravy went everywhere. And, poor Sarah you should have seen her face. She just dropped her tray and ran out of the cafeteria crying. It was just terrible. Everybody was looking and laughing. So-o-o embarrassing."

"Did anyone say anything?" Taylor asked.

"What?" the girls asked in unison.

"Why would anyone say anything? "After all, it was an *accident*" Amy said making air quotation marks.

"Yeah, some accident," Taylor replied sarcasm dripping from her words. Someone should have said…"

A tug on her backpack caused Taylor to turn around right into Marcie's face.

"Hey Marcie," Taylor spoke a slight tremor to her voice.

"Said something about what?" Marcie asked an evil grin on her face. "So, I guess your "friends" here been telling you about what happened in the cafeteria yesterday?"

"No, they weren't. Why don't you tell me what happened?" Taylor said cocking her head to the side completely ignoring the wide-eyed look of disbelief on Amy's face.

Marcie looked to the other girls standing near Taylor then back at Taylor. When the other girls would not look at her, Marcie answered.

"My girl April here accidently bumped into a friend of yours and made quite a mess. Spilled gravy and mashed potatoes all over the poor girl."

"It was corn," Amy corrected.

"My bad," Marcie said, the whole time her eyes fixed on Taylor's face. "Corn, mashed potatoes. What does it matter? So embarrassing. Girl ran out of the cafeteria so quickly, she didn't even hear April apologize."

Taylor looked at April who appeared anything but apologetic.

"Yeah," April replied feigning innocence, "she got out of there in such a hurry, she didn't even hear me say sorry."

"I bet you were sorry," Taylor replied.

"What, you callin me a liar?" April challenged, stepping closer to Taylor.

"Not now," Marcie warned stepping between April and Taylor pulling April away.

"We'll talk with you later," Marcie called out cheerily waving as she and her friends walked away.

"Hi girls," Angel greeted joining the group. "Everything alright over here?"

"Why wouldn't it be alright?" Taylor challenged.

"No reason," Angel replied taken aback by Taylor's response. "Just that from where I stood it looked like you and the other girl were into some sort of debate that looked like it was about to get physical."

"Well, nothing happened," Taylor shot back, "so you can be on your way."

"No, I can't," Angel replied a slight tremor in her voice as she tried to remain calm. "I have to talk with you."

"Why… and who are you anyway?" Taylor asked some of the bravado leaving her voice.

"My name is Angel and I'm a peer mentor, she identified herself extending her hand.

Taylor reluctantly accepted Angel's handshake. "What do you want with me?" she asked.

"You are Taylor Williams? Angel asked. In response to Taylor nodding her head in acknowledgment, Angel continued; "Ms. Foster said I was to meet with you today. Seems your friend Sarah had an incidence with April in the cafeteria."

"Yeah, I heard about that," Taylor replied giving the two other girls a censoring look before returning her gaze to Angel. "So, what does that have to do with you wanting to talk with me? I wasn't even at school yesterday."

"I know," Angel replied; "but Sarah says we should talk to you that this is not the first time you and your group, Angel indicated the other girls "have been the recipient of Marcie and her groups' accidents," she finished emphasizing accidents.

Taylor sighed heavily, holding onto the straps of her backpack she said:

"Okay, I'll talk with you." When do you want to talk?"

"Let's meet at lunch time, Angel answered. See that table out there by the big tree. We'll meet there."

"But isn't that where those weird girls meet?" Taylor asked.

"If you mean me and my friends, then yes," Angel answered matter-of-factly.

"I don't know," Taylor responded.

"What is there to know," Angel replied. "Either you will meet me there at lunch with my *weird friends* or we can meet in the principal's office. It's your choice. Which will it be?"

Taylor hesitated only for a moment longer before giving her reply.

"I'll see you at lunch."

The bell rang signaling the start of class. Angel watched Taylor and her group walk away. She couldn't suppress the smile of satisfaction as she turned to walk across the courtyard.

"Taylor Williams," she thought, *"you just don't know how weird!"*

* * *

46

The hurrieder, I go, the behinder I get became Angel's motto for the next two days. No matter how much she tried to be on time, she was constantly being sidetracked by something or someone. Today had been no exception. She hadn't been in the best of moods since Taylor was a no show to their meeting. Trying as hard as she could, Angel had been unable to catch even a glimpse of Taylor. She had tried arriving at the Quad early, but Taylor was a no show there. The other places she checked also turned up empty. She had decided when they did meet up, she would give Taylor a piece of her mind and then tell Ms. Foster, she was finished, and she wanted nothing else to do with Taylor Williams.

Angel entered the empty Quad, deciding to take a short cut through the locker corridor in hopes of getting to class before the late bell rang. She was feeling especially irritated at missing prayer with the girls and was so intent on getting to class that she did not see the backpack lying on the corridor floor until she tripped over it. Catching herself before falling, she looked down to see her foot caught in the back strap of a black and pink backpack.

"What, the..." She observed, releasing her foot from the backpack. Who would leave a backpack in the middle of the locker corridor? Looking down the corridor, she saw papers, books, pencils and other school supplies scattered down the corridor ending at an open locker. For a moment, she debated whether to investigate further but the sound of the late bell settled the matter for her. She had ten minutes. Quickly she began picking up the contents spilled from the backpack. A name scrawled across one of the sheets of paper caught her attention. Taylor is a ... had been written over the crude drawing of a large pig. Angel looked at the other sheets that looked as though they had been pulled from lockers and tossed onto the ground. She even found a couple of lockers that still held the offensive papers.

Arriving at the locker, she stopped as she came face-to-face with a larger sign that contained the same message as the smaller sheets.

"Hey," a voice called from behind her; "Where you going with my bag?"

Angel did not recognize the voice, but the silhouette appeared somewhat familiar. As the girl approached, recognition dawned.

"Taylor," Angel asked. "What happened?"

"What does it look like?" Taylor replied sarcastically. "I'll take my bag if you don't mind."

Angel handed the bag to Taylor. "I asked you what happened?" Angel repeated taking in Taylor's disheveled appearance, torn blouse, tear streaked face and red nose.

"Nothing, that concerns you," Taylor replied turning to her locker. Grunting at the sight of the offensive paper on her locker, she ripped it from the locker tearing it to pieces.

"Taylor," Angel spoke softly, "whatever is going on, I can help you. I told you that the other day when you were supposed to meet me and my friends for lunch."

"Yeah, about that...," Taylor began, shrugged her shoulders and grew silent staring intently into her locker.

"Is everything there?" Angel asked.

"What, I don't know," Taylor replied, "and I really don't care. I'm so tired of all of this." She sighed deeply, slumping against the locker.

"Come on we're going to the principal's office right now," Angel directed.

"It won't do any good," Taylor replied tears welling up in her eyes. "Nobody cares and anyway all the kids think I deserve whatever is happening to me because I betrayed my friend."

"I don't care about any of that," Angel spoke in a firm voice. "We're going to the principal right now and put a stop to all of this."

Seeing Taylor's resistance, Angel linked her arm with Taylor's and forced her to go with her.

"Hey Taylor," a girl Angel recognized as one of the girls that had been with Marcie the day before greeted them as they entered the office.

Taylor's eyes momentarily widened in surprise, but she quickly recovered before answering.

"Hey," Taylor mumbled in greeting. Turning to Angel, she pulled her arm from Angel and in a raised and angry voice said: "I told you I was alright and that I didn't want to come to the principal's office, so why are you dragging me in here?"

"What seems to be the problem girls," the secretary, Mrs. Stewart, asked coming to the counter. Dismissing the girl that greeted Taylor, she focused her stern gaze on Angel.

"Angel," she spoke recognizing her. "What is this all about? Aren't you girls supposed to be in class?

"Yes, Mrs. Stewart" Angel answered the principal's secretary, "but I...I mean we need to see the Principal, Ms. Mallard."

"Concerning what?" Mrs. Stewart asked eyeing the girls from over the rim of her glasses which had fallen off the bridge of her nose and were now perched on its tip.

Angel reached into her backpack and retrieved the stack of papers.

"These," she stated, presenting the offending papers for Mrs. Stewart's inspection.

"I see," Mrs. Stewart carefully looked over the pictures. "I take it you must be...Taylor," she continued pushing her glasses into place and staring at Taylor.

Angel was surprised when Taylor did not answer, but rather focused her gaze away from the secretary.

"Yes, this is Taylor," Angel supplied. "Now can we see the principal?"

"I'm not sure that will be necessary," Mrs. Stewart answered watching Taylor. "It doesn't appear that **Taylor**, she emphasized the name, is concerned or even has a complaint. Is that right, Taylor?

"I told her before she dragged me in here that, I didn't want to come," Taylor finished glaring at Angel.

"Is that true, Angel?" Mrs. Stewart asked. "You forced her to come?"

"Not exactly," Angel stammered.

"Either you did, or you didn't," Mrs. Stewart replied. "And, Angel, if you did in fact force this student to come to the office I will have to speak with your Coordinator."

"But, Mrs. Stewart," Angel tried to explain, "I found those posters spread out all over the locker corridor and..."

"It's settled," Mrs. Stewart said, holding her hand up to emphasize her words; "Taylor has said she did not want to come to the office to make a complaint or speak with the principal. Looking at the clock then back at Angel she continued; "By the way, you only have a few minutes to get to class before you will be considered absent for the day. If you hurry, I'm sure you can make it. With that she turned dismissing the girls and walked back to her desk taking the stack of papers with her.

Sitting at her desk, she tossed the papers into the trash, adjusted her glasses, and went back to work mumbling to herself that the principal had more important things to deal with than *girls being girls.*

Angel eyed the girl standing at the filing cabinet who had been watching the whole exchange. A crooked smile pulled at the corner of her mouth. When she realized Angel was watching, she quickly ducked her head pretending to be looking for something in the filing cabinet.

As soon as Angel was sure they would not be overheard after leaving the principal's office, she turned to Taylor.

"What was that all about? I thought you wanted to go see the principal about what happened."

Taylor stopped. Giving Angel a hard look she answered.

"NO, I didn't want to go to the principal's office. That was your idea, remember."

"Yeah, but you went with me," Angel defended.

"I didn't have much choice now did I seeing you grabbed my arm and all."

"I didn't grab your arm. I put my arm through yours."

"You call it what you want. It was your idea and you didn't give me much of a choice. Same thing you did the other day in the Quad. You just assumed I needed your help. You didn't bother asking me. Just so we are clear, I didn't then, and I don't need your help now that is. So, why don't you go and…bully someone else…or, I will go to the principal… about you. I'm sure Mrs. Stewart would love that!"

Turning abruptly Taylor walked away leaving Angel to stare after her.

"Hey girl, close your mouth," came a familiar voice.

"Eve," Angel breathed in relief. "Girl am I glad to see you!

You will not believe the morning I'm having!"

"Wanna bet?" Eve chuckled. "Why do you think I'm here? When you didn't show for prayer, I was concerned and then when you weren't in class, I figured something was wrong, so I got permission to leave class and came looking for you."

"I'm glad you came," Angel replied as a sigh escaped her lips.

"So, I gather from what I saw and overheard. You can thank me later," Eve giggled. "Right now, we gotta get to class." With that she linked her arm with Angel's, and they set off down the corridor at a brisk pace.

Angel found it hard to concentrate on classes as her mind kept returning to her encounter with Taylor. She briefly voiced her concerns to the girls at lunch but when they wanted to talk more about it, she said she didn't want to at that time. However, she asked if they could pray for Taylor. Each agreed to do so.

Two days later, Angel was surprised to find Taylor waiting for her in the Quad. She was alone and looked very uncomfortable.

"Does that offer to meet with you and your friends still stand?" Taylor asked.

"You sure you want to do that?" Angel asked wary of Taylor's seemingly change of heart.

"I'm sure, Taylor replied. "I owe you an apology about the other day. I was…well let's just say, I wasn't myself."

"I don't know anything about you being yourself or not," Angel replied. "All I know is you were like a Dr. Jekyll and Mr. Hyde."

"I've been told, I can be like that," Taylor answered color infusing her cheeks. "Would you accept my apology? "I promise, I won't act like that again."

"Alright. I accept your apology," Angel said still wary of Taylor. "If you want to meet with me and my friends be at the locker corridor at noon and you and I can go to the spot together."

"Okay, I'll see you at noon," Taylor agreed and walked away.

Chapter 5

"Hey everyone," Angel greeted as she came to the table. "Meet Taylor Williams. Taylor, these are my friends, the blonde there is Chris, and the one with the pencil stuck behind her ear is Sadie. That's Eve with the long black hair and the one with the freckles is Jade."

"Don't forget me," Mia chimed in.

"You cannot be forgotten," Angel joked good naturedly. "This is Mia."

"Hello," Taylor mumbled dropping her eyes.

"Come on sit down," Mia invited patting the open space beside her, "we were just about to get started."

"Get started with what?" Taylor asked eyeing them suspiciously.

"Lunch…what else?" Mia answered with a mischievous grin.

"Oh, okay," Taylor replied sounding relieved. Maybe they weren't as weird as she had heard. Taking her sandwich from her backpack she quickly unwrapped it and took a bite while the girls around her bowed their heads giving thanks. Looking from one girl to the next she began feeling uncomfortable. Shrugging her shoulders, she stopped chewing and bowed her head joining them.

"Amen," Mia concluded. "Amen," the others said in unison.

"Now," Eve asked, "Taylor what brings you to our little circle?"

"I didn't have a choice," Taylor replied munching on her sandwich ignoring the questioning looks of the girls.

Realizing Taylor was not going to give any further explanation, Angel began speaking looking from one girl to the next.

"That's not quite true. Taylor was given a choice; and she stood me up as you all know. I was surprised when she caught up with me this morning and asked if my invitation to join us for lunch was still open?"

"Interesting," Eve said nodding her head a wide smile on her face. "Seems prayer changes things."

"I don't understand," Taylor replied.

"It's like this," Eve explained. "When you stood our girl Angel up, she asked us to pray and we did…and… here you are."

"I still don't get it," Taylor responded, "but whatever. If you want to believe 'prayer' brought me here, so be it. But just so you know, my mother insisted I meet with you."

"Enough with that," Mia broke in, "I want to know about the in-ci-dent."

"Oh, that," Angel began. "Taylor do you want to tell them, or do you want me to tell them?"

"I'll tell them," Taylor replied. "It all began about a week ago when this girl Marcie came over to tell me about an accident in the cafeteria between my friend Sarah and her friend April. I asked if it really was an accident and I guess April got offended because she said I called her a liar. Then she moved in real close to me and Marcie steps between us. Then in a real friendly LOUD voice tells me she will talk with me later. At first I didn't know what was happening until the peer mentor here – she indicates Angel- shows up."

"I'd say it's a good thing Angel came when she did," Chris said.

"Maybe, but it didn't stop anything," Taylor replied.

"So, did something else happen?" Chris asked.

"Didn't your friend here tell you?" Taylor asked sounding defensive and casting a wary glance in Angel's direction.

"No," Eve defended Angel, 'our friend' as you call her did not tell us anything about what happened, but like I told you, she did ask us to pray for you."

Taylor looked at Angel. Anybody else would not have been able to keep what happened to themselves.

"You didn't tell?" Taylor stated turning her gaze upon Angel.

"No, I didn't."

"But, how could you not? Taylor asked. "Such a juicy piece of gossip. Why you would have been one of Marcie's best friends."

"You're real strange," Angel replied. "Why would I go around telling everyone about what was obviously a painful experience for you. Just so I could be…. what, friends with Marcie? Who is Marcie anyway?"

Feeling uncomfortable by Angel's words, Taylor shrugged her shoulders then answered; "Well all the girls I know would have given anything to have been witness to what you saw."

Angel shook her head, "If you haven't noticed, I'm not like all the girls you know. In fact, she indicated the girls sitting around the table, none of us are. Whatever you say to us will stay within this group, unless we believe not telling will bring harm to you, or someone else."

Tears sprang unexpectedly into Taylor's eyes. Looking into the concerned faces of the girls assembled around her, she spoke as the tears started running down her cheeks.

"I wish I could talk about it. But, talking will do no good. Those girls, they are just going to keep coming after me and my friends until…, well I don't know until what." Taylor finished the frustration evident in her voice.

"It doesn't have to be that way," Eve added.

"Are you serious?" Taylor asked raising her hands in exasperation. "Who or what is going to stop them from bothering me? The principal sure isn't, and well my friends are scared to do anything because they think Marcie and her friends will just come after us again. And, considering what happened to me and with what happened to Sarah…let's just say they will never say anything."

The girls looked from one to the other. Finally, Angel asked:

"So, you want to tell us what happened the other morning?"

Taylor shifted uncomfortably, looked from one girl to the other. "If you don't mind, I would rather not talk about that just now."

"That's fine with us," Chris said. "But, can you tell us why this girl Marcie and her group are after you?"

"It's a long story," Taylor began shifting in her seat, "and one I'm not very proud of."

"Don't worry about that," Mia assured her, "we have all done some things we are not very proud of, so you're in good company."

Taylor looked from one girl to the next trying to determine if they were sincere or not. Could they be trusted? How many times had she trusted other girls only to have that trust broken? Look at the mess she was in with Marcie after being so confident that they were the best of friends. But these girls seemed different…. Real. That was the word she was looking for "real." For the first time in a long time, she felt "safe." Going with her feelings and taking a deep breath, she plunged ahead.

"It started with me and Marcie. We were the best of friends since kindergarten that is until this year. We shared everything and when I say everything, I mean everything, clothes, make-up, shoes. You name it; we shared it. We would get together and talk about everything. At first, we only talked about girls we didn't like. You know, girls we thought dressed funny, or looked funny. But it was only between Marcie and me. She said I was her best friend and she could tell me anything. Then all that changed. Other girls joined the group and we would all get together and make comments about just about everybody. We would talk about the way they dressed, their hair and that kind of stuff. You know, harmless stuff. Then we would laugh whenever we passed them on campus. I wish I could say that is all we did but we didn't stop there, we would do little things, like 'accidentally' trip them up or maybe pull their backpack off. Once we even sent a girl a mean email.

We did some pretty awful stuff. My Mom kept trying to warn me that if Marcie did that to others it was only a matter of time before she did the same things to me. But what do mothers know, right? I wouldn't listen. I told her that Marcie and I were too good of friends and she would never talk about me with someone else."

The girls exchanged a knowing look as Taylor continued.

"Well, all that ended this year when Marcie started liking a boy in my homeroom. He and I were assigned to a group with four others as homework buddies. Marcie didn't believe me when I told her I didn't choose to be in the group, and that the teacher had assigned us to certain groups. She insisted that I liked the guy and was jealous because he liked her instead of me. She even accused me of bad mouthing her to him. I swore I hadn't and that I wouldn't do anything like that, but she didn't believe me.

That's when things really changed. Marcie started acting funny toward me. When I would try to join her and the group for lunch, she would ignore me, she stopped answering my calls, and she wouldn't email me back. Then one day I saw her in the locker corridor and tried to talk with her. She wouldn't listen; instead she loud talked me. Said I had betrayed her friendship and her trust. Then she turned her back on me and told her group that she couldn't stand a traitor. Said traitors needed to be punished. So, the group started calling me a traitor. She didn't even try to stop them. In fact, when she turned around to face me, she had this evil grin on her face. I was so hurt. How could she be so cold to me when we had been such good friends? I ran away and hung out in the restroom until school was over.

But I should have known it wasn't over. I returned to school the next day to kids I didn't even know talking about me saying I was a pig because I tried to steal my best friend's boyfriend. And, it continues. Marcie continues to spread lies about me, start rumors, harass me and my friends, and has even gone so far as to post a nasty note about me in the boys' gym.

At first, I just made up a bunch of excuses not to go to school. My mother wasn't going for it. She made me go and every day Marcie and her group would be waiting for me.

But, a few weeks ago, I came home, according to my Mom hysterical. And, after that, I guess I was acting weird and said some real stupid stuff because next thing I know my Mom is taking me to a counselor. I was doing pretty good after meeting with the counselor a few times until a week ago when Marcie and her group cornered me in the restroom. They surrounded me and pushed me against the wall. Even threatened to rip my clothes off. I believe they would have too if it had not been for a group of girls walking in at just that moment.

I got out of there as quick as I could. I knew I couldn't tell my Mom. She's been through enough with me already. And, this, well I don't think she can take anymore. So, when she asked me if I had met with my peer mentor, I thought about you, she said turning to Angel. You keep offering to help, so here I am."

Angel broke the silence that followed.

"I don't know about what Ms. Mallard is calling it *girls being girls*, sounds more to me like bull-y-ing."

"I agree," Sadie said. "After what you told us, this is gone way too far, and something needs to be done to put a stop to it! She finished slamming her fist into her open palm for emphasis.

"Yep, and we are just the ones to get the ball rolling," Mia declared rubbing her hands together relishing the thought of standing up for a fellow student.

"Look, I appreciate you girls wanting to help," Taylor replied, looking from one girl to the other; "but seriously, I don't think anyone can help. I started this mess. Like Ms. Mallard said, I am not innocent. I did the very same thing to other girls. Now that it's happening to me…well let's just say going to the principal seems like a wimpy thing to do…what is that saying…what you do to others comes back to you."

"I think it's do unto others as you would have others do unto you," Sadie supplied.

"Sounds more like what you sow you reap," Jade added.

"Yeah, yeah, all of that, Taylor replied, slumping her shoulders and furrowing her brow. I've done so much, and I guess what is happening to me is what I deserve."

"I don't think you or anyone else deserves being mistreated even if you did the wrong things in the past. And, as for going to the principal, I wouldn't call that wimpy, Eve added. "As a matter of fact, I think telling someone takes a lot of courage. You definitely would be sending a message to Marcie and her group or anyone else that's into bullying that you are tired of them mistreating you and you want it to S-T-O-P!"

"Well, when you put it that way," Taylor said sitting up and squaring her shoulders, "it doesn't sound wimpy at all. So, say I wanted to do something about Marcie and her group, what do you think I should do?"

"We can't tell you what to do," Angel answered, "but we can help you come up with some ideas and go with you to Principal Mallard's office."

Taylor's downcast eyes and frown indicated she was visibly shaken by the idea of going to Principal Mallard's office. Haltingly, she replied, "I don't know if I can do that. I already messed that up when I went to the office with you."

"I've got to admit," Angel said fixing her gaze on Taylor, "the way you acted when we went to Ms. Mallard's office caught me totally off guard. I wasn't expecting you to turn on me like that! But, I think if we go as a group, meaning all of us, she indicated the girls sitting around the table and your friends, Ms. Mallard will have to listen to what you tell her."

"Yeah," Mia interjected, "you won't be by yourself. We'll be with you!"

"That's right," Sadie added. "It won't be so easy to turn away a whole group of us!"

Taylor looked at the girls assembled around her, her eyes again filling with tears. She shook her head in amazement. Never had she experienced this type of support before; the kind that asked nothing of her in return. In the past, each time support had come it came with her having to do something in return. And, usually that something was against someone else. Especially being a part of Marcie's group. Even now she could feel the color rising in her cheeks as she thought about some of the mean things she had done to others. Sitting here amongst these girls, she wished she could take back the things she had done to hurt others. But she knew that was a useless wish. What had been done was done. She couldn't go back and undo it. But maybe by going to Principal Mallard, she could prevent some other girl from going through what she was going through. Maybe, it was worth a try. She just wasn't quite sure.

"Well, what do you say?" Angel spoke interrupting her thoughts.

"Umm, I don't know," Taylor hesitated bringing her focus back to the girls seated around her. "I want to...but. Let me think about it. Today is Friday. That gives me two days to think about it. Tell you what, I'll meet you all here on Monday, and I'll give you my answer. Okay?"

The girls looked from one to the other.

"Are you sure you don't want to go today?" Angel asked.

"Well, yeah, I'm sure," Taylor answered looking away from Angel's probing gaze.

"If that's your decision, we'll just have to wait until Monday then," Angel agreed swallowing her disappointment. Looking to the girls she silently asked for their agreement. Reluctantly, they nodded their heads in agreement.

The bell sounded signaling lunch was over and stopping any further discussion. Hastily the girls gathered up their things. Taylor grabbed her backpack, falling in step with Sadie, Mia, and Jade as they headed to class.

We didn't pray, Angel thought, as she waved good-bye to Eve and Chris, heading in the opposite direction to her next class, all the while trying to ignore the strange feeling that came over her.

* * *

Bidding her friends good-bye and telling them she would see them on Monday, Taylor made her way home. She had told her mother she was walking home with her friends but since meeting with Angel and her group, she had a lot to think about. Rather than going for ice cream, Taylor decided to use this time to think about what she was going to do about the Marcie situation.

All afternoon she had been nervous and jumpy after her meeting with Angel and her friends, thinking somehow Marcie would know what she had been talking about and do something to punish her for her betrayal. Even when she shared with her friends what had happened that afternoon, she kept looking over her shoulder to make sure neither Marcie, nor one of her spies, was within ear shout. Now, with only two blocks from home, she allowed herself to relax, letting her mind wander back to the events of the afternoon focusing on her lunch with Angel and the other girls.

She had enjoyed herself, despite her earlier misgivings. They were different she concluded adjusting her backpack, not weird. It didn't take long for her to realize that the lunch hour would not be spent gossiping about fellow students or even in idle chit-chat about the goings on of the latest reality stars. Their meeting had begun with prayer. She was relieved when they did not try to force her to join them but had allowed her to make up her mind if she wanted to or not. When she chose to start eating, they did not make a big deal of it, just went on prayed, said amen and continued their conversation as though nothing out-of-the-ordinary had happened.

Even now she smiled recalling the light bantering between Sadie and Jade. Each one was so different from the other but they all seemed to get along quite nicely. She was surprised to discover that she liked them and felt she could trust them. There was something peaceful about being around them and she looked forward to their next meeting.

In the meantime, she had a big decision to make. Her steps slowed as she pondered what she should do. Would she take the girls' up on their offer and go to Ms. Mallard, or would she silently continue to endure the attacks from Marcie and her group? She didn't want to be labeled a whimp, a snitch, or even a coward as was sure to happen once Marcie's spy in the principal's office got the word out. Yeah, Marcie had a spy in the principal's office; a bit of information she had not shared with Angel when she had escorted her to the office. The thought of Marcie learning of her going to the principals' office sent a cold shiver down her back. She knew Marcie would be after her, even though she didn't say anything to Ms. Mallard. She wished there was some other way.

Why couldn't she just wake up tomorrow and find everything back like it was before the "boy." Or, maybe she could fake some kind of illness that would keep her from having to attend school until next year. Naw, she shook her head at the thought. That would never do. She had already ditched classes more than she wanted anyone to know, especially her mother and her grades had fallen below grade level. Another bit of information, she had been withholding. At this point, it would take a miracle for her to pull her grades up enough for her to advance to the next grade. She knew it was only a matter of time before administration made her Mom aware of her absences from school and her failing grades. She knew her Mom would be devastated. And the thought of disappointing her mother caused her to slow her pace even more.

She realized that she had only one choice…talk to her mother when she got home. As she turned the corner, her house came into view. Sighing deeply, she resigned herself to talk with her Mom and maybe she would take the girls up on their offer to go with her to report Marcie and her crew.

"Might as well get it over with," she mumbled to herself taking in a deep breath. Her decision made, she adjusted her backpack and picked up her pace.

The sound of running footsteps caused her to turn to see who was coming up behind her. As she did so, two girls collided with her knocking her off balance and sending her crashing to the ground. With a screech of surprise, she tried to put her hands in front of her dislodging her backpack strap from one shoulder. The loose backpack bounced against her chest and thudded to the ground. She threw out her hands, trying to break her fall but they gave way under her weight. Her face crashed onto the backpack, bounced off and hit the cement. The distorted sound of giggling was the last thing she heard as blackness engulfed her.

Chapter 6

Streaks of lightening flashed across the dark and ominous sky followed shortly by the rumble of thunder as the threat of the impending storm moved over the school. Giants carrying huge clubs stomped through the campus crushing buildings and students in their wake leaving chaos and confusion as they went. Students cried out, their shrieks of fear and anguish filled the air. Angel stood alone away from the chaos on the main part of campus. Unable to move, she struggled to free herself of the chains holding her captive.

One giant seeing her struggling left the group and started towards her, the ground shaking with each step. He had a crazed look on his face which was distorted by his grotesque grimace of a smile. Angel struggled harder trying to get loose. As the giant approached closer, he raised his huge club preparing to strike. Angel was terrified wanting to run but couldn't. She screamed as the huge club was coming down.

"Angel, Angel, wake up," Amber called shaking her sister.

"What?" Angel asked jerking awake still remembering the terrifying dream, her breathing as though she had been running, her heart pounding, sweat at her temples and on her upper lip.

"Giants," she cried still not free of her dream.

"Angel wake up," Amber demanded continuing to shake her sister. "They're calling you."

"What?" Angel asked coming awake looking around wildly.

"It's for you," Amber informed her. "It's Eve. She's on the phone. Says it's important!"

Angel fully awake now grabbed her robe and ran into the kitchen to answer the phone.

"Get ready. We'll be picking you up in 20 minutes," Eve spoke as soon as Angel said hello. "Something has happened to Taylor. She's in the hospital."

"What?" Angel gasped.

"No time to explain just be ready!" Eve said.

Hurriedly Angel hung up the phone and dashed back into her room to throw on a pair of sweats, pile her curls into a high pony, splash cold water on her face and quickly brush her teeth before heading for the door. Her mother was in the kitchen enjoying a leisurely cup of coffee while browsing the Saturday paper. She looked up as Angel burst into the kitchen.

"Mom," Angel threw over her shoulder heading for the backdoor, "Eve called, seems one of the girls we were working with is in the hospital and we're on our way up there."

"Oh dear," her mother replied. "I hope everything is alright. Do you need me and Amber to come with?"

"No, Mom," Angel threw over her shoulder as she rushed out the door; "but some prayer would help."

"We will do that."

"What happened?" Angel asked as soon as she entered the van. "Why is Taylor in the hospital?"

Ms. Foster reminded Angel to buckle her seatbelt staving off her questions as she eased the van into the street before she began relaying the story to the girls just as Mrs. Williams had told her.

"Well according to Taylor's Mom, Taylor was walking home from school alone when she was pushed from behind by a couple of girls that laughed and ran off. Thankfully, a woman driving down the street saw everything and stopped to help Taylor. When she got to Taylor, she discovered she was unconscious and bleeding, so she called the police and the police called the ambulance.

Taylor's Mom heard all the sirens and went outside to see what was going on and see if she could be of assistance as she is a nurse. When she got to the child laying on the sidewalk and discovered it was Taylor lying there in a pool of blood, she said she almost lost it. Fortunately, she was able to hold it together while the paramedics assisted Taylor and took her to the hospital. She didn't ride to the hospital with Taylor but chose to take her own vehicle. Before she left, she called Taylor's father and me to let us know what had happened.

When she arrived at the hospital, doctors were already attending to Taylor. They assured her their preliminary examination showed Taylor would be alright, but they would be taking x-rays just to be sure. The doctor's discovered Taylor had a concussion and her nose was broken and her lips busted which accounted for all the blood. She needed a few stitches but fortunately, she didn't lose her front teeth. Said, she would have a couple of black eyes from the nose injury, but the doctor had assured Mrs. Williams, Taylor should be ready to go home in a few days.

"Thank God," Mia breathed.

"Poor kid," Sadie sympathized.

"Pushed from behind," Angel repeated in amazement. "Who would do such an awful thing?"

"That's what the police are trying to determine," Ms. Foster answered. "The witness gave a pretty good description of the girls and from what Mrs. Williams tells me, the police believe the girls attend Carver Preparatory. But they can't be sure. They will be talking with students to help them find the persons that did this."

"Wow," Jade spoke up. "This seems really serious, calling in the police and all."

"Yes, Jade, this is serious," Ms. Foster replied. "Taylor was injured quite badly and if it had not been for that woman, it is no telling how long she would have lain on the sidewalk without medical attention. Taylor is very fortunate there are still some people in this world that don't mind getting involved."

"Ms. Foster," Sadie volunteered, "we just met with Taylor yesterday at lunch. There were some things going on, but she wasn't willing to talk to us about them. Do you think the police would like to know that?"

"Yeah," Chris added, "she said she didn't want to talk about them right now, even when we tried to get her to talk."

"But, Angel knows," Eve interjected.

"What are you talking about?" Ms. Foster questioned.

"Angel knows," Eve explained. "She tried to get Taylor to tell us about what happened a few days ago but Taylor wouldn't. And…"

"Wait, a minute," Ms. Foster interrupted. "Eve, did I hear you correctly? Are you saying Angel knew Taylor might have been in danger and didn't tell anyone?"

"No!" Eve quickly corrected, "not that Taylor might have been in danger but that something happened that she needed to tell somebody about. In fact, she took Taylor to the principal's office, but Taylor acted all strange and refused to say anything."

Ms. Foster cast a glance at Angel who was looking intently out the window as they pulled into the hospital parking lot. Finding a spot, Ms. Foster parked. Angel made to get out of the van, but Ms. Foster stopped her.

"Angel," Ms. Foster spoke her voice firm, "before we go in to see Taylor you need to tell us what has been going on."

Angel turned from the window, her eyes meeting those of Ms. Foster. How could she explain all that had been going on since getting this assignment? First the old memories of her own bullying had left her weak and feeling vulnerable, a feeling she intensely did not like. Then there were the feelings of being optimistic because she thought she was making progress with Taylor when she agreed to meet with her only to have those feelings dashed when Taylor didn't show up. It was bad enough that she was feeling like a total failure and if that wasn't enough she had this strange feeling because they had not prayed after meeting with Taylor. And, how could she forget, the dreams!

As she looked at Ms. Foster, the emotions welled up taking hold of her. With a shaky breath, she tried to speak but was unable to do so. Her words seemed to have all come together and formed a lump in her throat making speech impossible. She raised her hand placing it on her throat, as tears filled her eyes and began flowing down her cheeks. With a resigned shrug of her shoulders, Angel dropped her head cradling it in her hands began to weep loudly. Everyone was silent. The only sound was that of Angel's sobs. Mia being closest reached her hand over the seat and gently patted Angel's shoulder.

"This... this... is... too... much... for... me," Angel struggled to push the words past the lump in her throat, her weeping having subsided enough for her to speak.

"What is too much for you, Angel?" Ms. Foster asked, placing her finger under Angel's chin coaxing her to look up.

"This assignment," Angel chocked turning her red splotched face up to Ms. Foster. "I'm no good at this. Chris was better suited for it and she wanted it, but you gave it to me knowing my past. Why you would give this assignment to me… it's not fair. How could you do this? Now Taylor is in the hospital and it's all… my… fault!" Angel wailed looking into Ms. Foster's eyes.

"Angel, Angel," Ms. Foster spoke softly breaking through Angel's wailing. Although awkward, Ms. Foster gathered Angel into her arms and gently began to rock her. She looked to the girls to indicate that they should pray, but they were already doing so, hands joined together, lips moving in a silent plea for their friend. Ms. Foster continued to cradle Angel and rock her until her wailing subsided. Sniffling, Angel pulled away from Ms. Foster.

Does anyone have a tissue? Ms. Foster asked.

"I don't need one," Angel answered. Reaching into her pocket she retrieved a freshly laundered hankie. She blew her nose and sat quietly, looking out the window. Slowly her sniffling subsided.

"I'm… sorry," Angel mumbled. "What no wise cracks?" she chided turning to the girls her eyes resting on Mia. Mia looked back at Angel, her own tears glistening off her cheeks. She reached out and touched Angel's arm as she solemnly shook her head. Angel looked to the other girls. Eve wiped the tears from her cheeks and Chris gave her a watery wink. Sadie pressed her hands to her heart and Jade who had obviously been crying loudly blew her nose.

Angel turned to Ms. Foster, her eyes searching for what she could not say. Then she realized what it was she was looking for— disapproval. That was it. Disapproval but there was none. Her eyes moved from Ms. Foster to the girls surrounding her. All gave her the same look—love. She could feel it as if it were a tangible thing. Each one drew her into the circle of their love and covered her as she struggled to gain her balance. Feeling bolstered by the love surrounding her, Angel let out a deep sigh before beginning.

"I was bullied," Angel's voice shook. Swallowing loudly, she began again. But, right now Taylor needs us, and well, if you will all bear with me a little longer, I promise I will tell you all about it at our next meeting. "Will that be alright with you?" she asked directing her question to Ms. Foster.

Ms. Foster hesitated before speaking, "I agree with you that we are here for Taylor but," she paused, "we have all been very concerned about you. It will be up to the girls to decide if they are willing to let you off the hook, so to speak."

"I don't know," Mia was the first to speak up. "You aren't in the best of shape and what if you go in there and, well… fall apart?"

"I won't fall apart," Angel replied.

"You might think you won't fall apart, but this has been pretty painful for you Angel," Sadie responded. "I hate to see you in such pain, and maybe if you talk about it, some of that pain will leave. It must have been pretty horrible for you."

Everyone went silent, eyes fixed on Angel. Cocking her head to the side, eyes cast down, Angel weighed her next words carefully.

"I'm so lucky… no blessed," she corrected a small smile on her face, "to have such wonderful friends, and you Ms. Foster. You are all so concerned about me and … well, I am so thankful for your… caring but believe me, I am okay. I don't know how to explain it, but… well it's like that… heaviness that has been on me… is well… gone. I feel stronger! Like I'm ready to go into battle… does that make sense," she giggled.

"Makes perfect sense to me," Sadie answered. "That's prayer power!"

"Yeah, Angelica," Chris teased. "What do you think we've been doing this whole time that you've been acting strange?"

"Girl," Eve laughed, "strange is not the word for it. Remind us to tell you about yourself at our next meeting. In the meantime, it's time for us to get busy on this Mission Him- Possible!"

"Ready!" Chris exclaimed.

"Wait, wait," Angel stopped them, "we've got to pray first!"

"Of course, silly," Chris agreed. "We can't go into battle without…."

"Prayer Power!" they chorused.

Angel was first to arrive at Taylor's hospital room. She stopped abruptly just inside the door as her eyes fell on the small figure lying in the hospital bed. Although Ms. Foster had tried describing Taylor's appearance, she was not prepared for what she saw. She heard Mia gasp close beside her. Unable to believe what she was seeing, she turned eyes wide in disbelief looking to Ms. Foster.

This couldn't possibly be Taylor she thought as her eyes swung back to the person lying in the bed. She had just seen her. There must be some mistake. Maybe they got the room numbers mixed up. Ms. Foster said Taylor was pushed? How could a push do so much damage?

Ms. Foster seeing the color drain from Angel's face made her way to Angel and wrapped her arm around her shoulder. Angel's body sagged against Ms. Foster.

"Angel are you alright?" she asked her voice full of concern.

Angel only shook her head no. She was not prepared to see Taylor in this condition.

"Do you want to step outside for a minute?" Again, Angel could only nod, yes.

Ms. Foster supported Angel from the room and allowed the other girls to go in. She whispered that they should not try to talk with Taylor as she needed her rest.

"We won't," Eve assured Ms. Foster. "We'll just pray and leave."

"Yeah," Mia added, "and we won't pray loud or long."

Chris thoughtfully eyed the obviously shaken Angel leaning against Ms. Foster.

"You sure you don't want to come in and pray with us?" she asked.

Angel's answer was to drop her head and shake it no. Had Ms. Foster not been holding on to her, she was sure she would have run from the hospital at that moment.

"Angel," Ms. Foster began, "lets you and I pray for Taylor."

"I can't," Angel whispered loudly. "This is my fault. I'm sure God doesn't want to hear from me." With that she pulled away from Ms. Foster and bolted down the corridor.

"Young lady, no running," the desk nurse reprimanded.

Reaching the elevator, she pressed the button. Too agitated to wait for the car, she headed toward the stairs. Holding onto the rail Angel sped down the three flights of stairs, pushed open the double glass doors exiting the hospital, leaving the sights and smells behind her.

Spying a fountain in the center of the courtyard, she made her way to a bench, covered her face and began to weep. The picture of Taylor would not leave her mind. She had looked so small and frail. Her head wrapped in white gauze looked like a Q- Tip. The thick gauze and tape across her nose left the dark purple bruises around her eyes in stark contrast. Her lips were puffy and distorted, and she could see the stitches used to close the cuts made by Taylor's teeth. Her hands lay motionless, two puffy white balls of bandages with tiny fingers sticking through them.

"Hey, Angel," Eve's voice interrupted her thoughts. Wrapping her arm around Angel's shoulder, she spoke. "I know she looks bad, but the doctor said she will be fine in a few weeks. Said she looks a lot worse than she is."

"Eve," Angel sobbed, collapsing against Eve's shoulder. "This is all my fault. We didn't pray. I knew we should have prayed, but I didn't insist. So much was going on…"

The others had gathered around Angel. Jade came to stand in front of Angel. Reaching out she took Angel's hand in hers, "Angel," she spoke softly but firmly. "What makes you think you could have changed what happened to Taylor?"

Angel raised a tear-streaked face to Jade, "Because, don't we always say prayer changes things?" If we prayed, maybe Taylor would not be in the hospital right now.

Or, maybe, Ms. Foster added, "Taylor could be in a worse shape than she is."

"I don't see how it could be any worse," Angel replied. "She looks terrible!"

"I know she looks terrible, but remember the doctor said she is not in as bad a shape as she looks."

"I feel just awful about what happened to her. I wish she would have trusted us enough to let us help her," Angel said shrugging her shoulders a forlorn look on her face.

Ms. Foster and the girls circled Angel in a group hug. They held her tightly. Chris broke the silence, "We all wish she would have let us help her. Maybe now, she will realize she needs help and will be more willing to let us help her."

"Yeah, just like someone else we know," Eve added.

Chapter 7

The meeting Angel promised to attend was proving to be more difficult than she thought. Entering the Sanctuary, she felt anxious and alone, feelings she hadn't experienced in a very long time. The dreams of the giants had persisted and each time, the giant would turn and come toward her, she found herself bound and unable to move or speak. All she wanted was for it to go away.

Angel had arrived early and began helping Ms. Foster prepare the snacks and set up for the tea. Thoughts of the past swirled around in her head causing her to only glance at the chicken, cranberry and crème cheese sandwiches cut into dainty squares minus the crust. When Ms. Foster offered her one of the sandwiches she loved so much, she declined. So, caught up in her thoughts, Angel barely noticed the delicious aroma from the fresh- baked scones filling the air. Not even the three-tiered tray laden with various bite-sized pastries could take her mind from her troubling thoughts. By the time the others arrived, everything was ready. Angel was a bundle of nerves anticipating sharing her story. She didn't know if she would be able to share as promised.

Today, there was no table between them. The larger conference table had been replaced by the smaller oval table Ms. Foster used when serving tea. Each girl took a seat in one of the high-backed chairs set in a semi-circle around the smaller table. Mia eyeing the three-tiered pastry tray, in the middle of the table rubbed her hands together in anticipation of the tasty treats.

"Ms. Foster is serving tea!" Jade exclaimed sitting up straight in her chair.

"How delightful!" Sadie said with her best British accent.

They loved tea with Ms. Foster. Ever since her return from Atlanta, she had made it a practice to serve tea at least once-a-month. She shared with the girls that the highlight of her trip to Atlanta had been the experience of high tea.

After everyone was seated, Ms. Foster greeted each one then disappeared momentarily. She returned pushing an intricately scrolled wrought-iron white tea cart. On it was a beautiful floral teapot with matching tea cups and saucers. A floral-patterned platter contained the fresh from the oven scones the girls had smelled upon entering the Sanctuary. Small crystal bowls each with its own small silver spoon, held an assortment of various jellies and clotted cream. Bowing their heads, they said grace. After, Ms. Foster served tea giving each girl a delicate floral printed porcelain plate and a scone. Amidst giggles and light banter, the girls munched their way through jellied scones and delicious hot tea with cream.

Angel gradually began to relax as she settled into the ritual of the formal tea. She took comfort in pouring cream from the small vintage silver pitcher lightly stirring her tea with the special silver tea spoon. Soon, her troubling thoughts disappeared as she focused her attention on the tea ritual. Holding the delicate saucer with her palm flat, lifting the cup with her fingers together being sure to not put her finger through the cup handle. Slowly bring the cup to her lips taking a sip of the hot, sweet creamy tea with a faint taste of lavender. By the time Ms. Foster served the delicate sandwiches, she was feeling a bit more like herself eating four of them and even joining in the conversation swirling around her.

"I'm glad you're feeling better," Mia observed.

"Yes, I am," Angel said. "Thank you, Ms. Foster, for the tea, and thank you all for putting up with me. I'm ready to share my story with you."

The girls sat their tea cups down, all eyes on Angel as she began to talk.

"I was bullied," Angel confessed." It got so bad that I did not want to go to school. But my mother would not hear of me not going to school. Said I needed to learn to stand up for myself and not let anyone push me around. That wasn't all, she told me the only way *those kids* would respect me was for me to stand up for myself. I wasn't looking for respect; I just wanted them to leave me alone. And, I knew, from experience standing up for myself would just make things worse. So, I ditched.

I wasn't alone. I quickly met up with a group of kids that ditched school like me. They didn't ask me a bunch of questions. They just accepted me, so I started hanging out with them. I 'changed' as my mother put it. She blamed it on the group of rough kids I was hanging with. She didn't know those rough kids kept me from being alone and unprotected. Since I was no longer alone, I was no longer an easy target.

For two years they were my protection. When I was with them, I didn't have to worry about being bullied. Looking back, I realize now it wasn't the best solution, but it was the only one I had at the time. I never talked about how I felt when I was bullied. I just suffered in silence. When I came to Ms. Foster, I mentioned it to her but since it had been so long ago, I thought I was over it. Then, along comes this assignment.

Remember how I acted that first day of the assignment? Well, it's done nothing but get worse and worse. I have these awful dreams. And when we left after meeting with Taylor without praying, I had this…this, I don't know it was a real strange feeling. I don't like the way I'm feeling or acting these days. I feel…I feel… I really don't know how to describe it. I'm scared, I'm angry, I'm ashamed, all rolled into one. I act one way at home, another with all of you, and another when it comes to Taylor.

Most of the time, I feel helpless especially when it comes to taking the lead on this assignment.

And, Taylor, well until two days ago, I felt Taylor hated me. I was ready to give up and then here she comes telling me she wants to meet with us. I really didn't expect her to show, so when she did, I was more than surprised." Angel hesitated to look to Ms. Foster who nodded her head for her to continue. "And... well, I haven't been, shrugging her shoulders and dropping her head she continued...praying. Figured what's the point. If God didn't hear me then... why would He hear me now?"

The room remained quiet after Angel finished speaking. Their silence made her uncomfortable. She wished someone would say something. Shifting uncomfortably in her chair, she waited, eyes downcast. Sadie broke the silence.

"Wow, Angel, what took you so long to share all this with us?"

Nothing could have prepared Angel for Sadie's response to her words. Jerking her head up, she looked intently into Sadie's eyes trying to figure out if she in fact heard what sounded like... concern.

"I don't know," Angel replied, weighing her words and looking from one girl to the next; "I...I, guess I didn't want you guys to know that I'm not as strong as you think I am."

"I don't understand," Mia spoke up. "What does being strong have to do with being bullied? Didn't we tell Taylor that there is nothing wrong with telling someone about being bullied? If it is okay for her, then why isn't it okay for you?"

"Because..." Angel stopped, let out a loud sigh, "I guess there is no difference," she admitted her voice dropping. "It's just that, well I was so ashamed. Every time I would think about those times the shame would overwhelm me. Then, I would get angry at myself for being so weak and helpless. So, I ran away. When I met Taylor, she had that same look. It was only for a moment, but I recognized it. It made me remember my own bullying experience. I didn't want to remember, so I got angry. When I had time to think about it, I remembered how I acted. I remembered wishing someone cared enough about me to look past all the angry words, the bad attitude and just help me. After that, I knew I couldn't run away and had to do everything possible to help Taylor. So, I determined that no matter how ugly Ms. Taylor acted, I would not run away but be there to help her when she decided she needed help.

A couple days after that first meeting, I saw Taylor in the locker corridor and she looked so…scared and hurt, I couldn't just leave her. I admit, I did get a little physical with her. But I knew how important it was for her to go to Principal Mallard's office, but when we got there, she turned on me. I'm not sure, but I think it had something to do with the girl that was working in the office."

"Is that all of it?" Ms. Foster asked when Angel finished speaking.

"Most of it," Angel answered.

"So, what now?" Eve asked. "What can we do to help you Angel?

"Me," Angel sounded surprised. "This is not about me; it's about Marcie and Taylor."

"Yeah, them too, but sounds more like you need our help before we can even think about helping anyone else" Eve replied.

"I agree with Eve," Sadie spoke up. "We've been talking to Ms. Foster about you ever since the first day of this assignment."

"What?" Angel exclaimed; "you've been talking about me behind my back?"

"Yes," Ms. Foster answered, "if by that you mean that the girls have been concerned about you and asked me what they could do to help you? Then yes, we have been discussing you, without your knowledge."

"See, Angel," Mia interjected. "There you go, getting angry and you don't even know why we talked to Ms. Foster about you in the first place. Instead of thinking it was because we love you and are concerned, you think we would bad mouth you. Why can't you just say thank you that we care enough about you to want to help you?"

"Yeah," Chris said, "we know this assignment cannot be easy on you. It wouldn't be easy for me or any one of us," she emphasized one while indicating the other girls. "But when we all join in together, well it makes it a lot easier to handle."

"Like the scripture that says…where two or three are joined together in my name, there I am in there with them," Jade paraphrased.

"It doesn't say that," Sadie corrected.

"I know," Jade said, "but I think Angel gets the message."

"Okay you two," Angel laughed, "don't get started. Thank you Jade, I do get the point. And Sadie, you're right, it doesn't say that, but I think it means that. Thank you all. And, please… HELP!"

"Then let's get started right now," Ms. Foster interjected sitting back in her chair, folding her hands in her lap and looking directly at Angel. "Angel is there anything else we need to know?"

The color rose in her cheeks. Shifting uncomfortably in her chair, she swallowed loudly before speaking.

"Well...I keep having this dream about giants," she said her eyes widening and her voice barely above a whisper as she began talking about the dream. "It's all dark and creepy. There's this storm going on with lots of thunder and lightning. We're all at school but I'm tied up and can't get loose. There are giants everywhere. Kids are running and screaming but there is no one that can stop the giants. They are going through the school smashing buildings and destroying everything in their sight. Then one of the giants turns and sees me struggling. I'm chained and can't get loose. He stops, laughs and starts coming toward me. He is huge and awful looking. He has this giant size club and a crazy look in his eyes like he can't wait to smash me with his club. The ground shakes with each step he takes and he's laughing this horrible laugh. I am so scared. I struggle, harder, trying to get free but I can't. I open my mouth to scream but nothing comes out! He's so close, and his club is coming down and... I wake up."

"That is some dream!" Mia exclaimed.

"I'll say," Ms. Foster agreed. "Are you alright? Would you like a drink of water?" she asked seeing that Angel had gone quite pale.

Angel could only nod her head yes in answer to Ms. Foster's question.

Jade jumped up to get a glass from the buffet. Quickly she poured cold water into the glass and took it to Angel who gratefully received the water glad to have finished telling them about her dream.

"Thank you Jade," Angel spoke between large gulps. Holding the empty glass, she looked from one girl to the next. All eyes were on her except for Sadie who seemed occupied writing in her notebook.

"Would you like more?" Ms. Foster asked.

Angel only shook her head remaining silent waiting for the girls to comment.

"Well?" Angel asked spreading her hands in exasperation.

"Well, what?" Chris replied. "Seems to me the whole thing is pretty clear."

"Clear?" Angel echoed, her brow wrinkled.

"Yes, clear," Eve joins in. "You've been trying to do this on you own, and well, it is too much for you."

"You mean…" Angel began.

"Yeah," Mia interrupted; "even a blind man can see your dream is about you."

"But, what about the storm and all? How can that possibly be about me?" Angel questioned.

"I think the storm is about this assignment and all the challenges you are having," Sadie answered. "Seems to me something deep inside is telling you not only this assignment, but your own bullying incidence are too much for you to handle."

"I don't know," Angel said shaking her head in disbelief, looking to Ms. Foster. "If it is about me, why can't I get free? After all, I am a member of the God Squad."

"Yes, you are a member of the God Squad," Ms. Foster answered, "but what is one of the important coverings of the God Squad?"

"What do they have to do with my dream?" I don't see what being transformed by the Word, empowered by the Holy Spirit, dressed for battle, and…"

The girls jumped to their feet, shouting in unison, "Prayer Power!" as they raised their hands in victory.

"Prayer Power," Ms. Foster repeated as the girls sat back down. "You are missing a part of your covering…prayer. You said yourself, you have not been praying. Leaving out prayer left you unprotected, and that is why in your dream, you are bound and not able to defend yourself against the giant."

"Wow, Ms. Foster," Angel exclaimed, her eyes filling with tears, "all the time I was thinking God wouldn't hear me because He didn't hear me back then, but I was wrong. I ran away from the bullies then, but mostly I ran away from God."

"Yes, child," Ms. Foster soothed; "when you stop praying, you put yourself in a very vulnerable position. If you don't pray, you are no longer in communication with God. At first you no longer hear Him clearly, or you question if that is Him speaking. But, if you don't stop and pray, you will continue to stumble along. After a while you find you have stumbled yourself right from under the covering and protection He provides because you can no longer hear His voice."

"Ms. Foster?" Angel questioned, tears streaming down her cheeks. "Have, I gone too far?"

"Child," Ms. Foster chuckled giving Angel's hand a reassuring pat. "No! God knows you better than you know yourself. He already knew you were going to get off track and made a way for you to get back on the right track. In other words, He has what I like to call a 'just in case clause' especially for times like these."

"He does?" Angel asked not understanding what Ms. Foster was getting at.

"The clause is not just for you but for all of us," she explained.

"I John 1:9," Chris volunteered.

"That's right Chris, you remembered," Ms. Foster smiled at her warmly. Taking the Bible from the bookshelf, she opened it before continuing.

"If we, she read slowly, admit that we have sinned and confess our sins, He is faithful and just, and will forgive our sins and get rid of the junk from all our wrongdoing, our bad behavior and everything not in line with His will and purpose."

"So, you see Angel," Eve said, "You haven't gone too far. All you need to do is tell God you messed up and ask Him to forgive you."

"Wait, a minute," Angel said, "you know about this clause too."

"Of course," Eve chuckled.

"We all do," Chris responded with a wink. "You're probably the only one that didn't know about it…ANGEL."

They all shared a hearty laugh before gathering into their prayer circle. Angel did not wait but began praying as soon as they all had joined hands.

"Father, thank you for Your 'just in case clause.' Forgive me for running away from you…"

Chapter 8

Angel entered the quiet hospital room where Taylor lay sleeping. The large bandages that covered Taylor's head when they first visited were gone. A smaller puffy square now covered the partially bruised area of her forehead. The bandage on her nose was gone leaving the dark bruising around Taylor's eyes visible. Angel could see the bruises were starting to fade and the swelling in her face was not so noticeable. Taylor was definitely improving after three days in the hospital.

Prior to coming to the hospital, Angel had talked to Taylor's mother. Mrs. Williams had assured her it would be alright for her to visit Taylor, and that Taylor would be released in the next day or so. She shared that Taylor was feeling down and that maybe she could give her a little encouragement.

"What a mess," Angel thought turning to look out the window. "If only...," shaking her head, she cleared her thoughts. If only thinking did no good. She had come to that conclusion after a long discussion with Ms. Foster and the girls. They assured her she did all within her power to help Taylor. They all tried to help? But, in the end the decision had rested with Taylor.

Yes, she did as much as Taylor would allow. In one instance she had even overstepped her authority as a peer mentor. The thought caused her to wince. She could not blame herself for what happened to Taylor she reasoned within herself. But the words did not make her feel any better. She would have to be satisfied that she had done as much as Taylor would let her do.

Turning, from the window, her gaze focused on Taylor who was grimacing as she adjusted her position. Not wanting to wake her,

Angel quietly sat in the chair beside Taylor's bed. Opening her small devotional, she began reading the topic for the day.... Giant Slayers! Scriptural reference Numbers 13th Chapter.

"What are you doing here?" Taylor asked startling Angel.

"Hey, glad you're awake," Angel replied.

"What are you doing here?" Taylor repeated.

"I came to see you."

"For what?" Taylor asked turning an indifferent eye to Angel.

"Well, for starters," Angel replied ignoring Taylor's comment; "we were all here the other day, and you didn't look so good. Doctor said you needed your rest, so we didn't stay. I came back because I wanted to make sure you were okay."

Taylor eyed Angel intently before speaking.

"You sure that's all?"

"Excuse me, I think I missed something," Angel said not understanding. "What other reason would I have to come here but to see how you're doing?"

"I don't know?" Taylor replied the frustration evident in her voice.

"Taylor, I didn't mean to upset you," Angel soothed surprised by Taylor's admission. "I, I,..."

Taylor raised her thickly bandaged hand, stopping Angel. "It's not you; it's me. So much has happened. I lay here and think about that day over and over. And, I get so angry. Then, I start getting down on myself because I didn't do anything when I had the chance. And, I feel so...so...ashamed."

"Ashamed?" Angel repeated.

Taylor turned her head, looking in Angel's eyes before continuing.

"Yes, ashamed. I realize now I, had the chance to do something before all this happened but I didn't. I wish I listened to you the day you took me to the office. I should have talked to Ms. Mallard but instead, I...I... was afraid. I was afraid Marcie would find out. Especially, when I saw one of the girls that hangs out with her in the office."

Seeing Angel's questioning look, Taylor explained.

"I know you wondered why I acted so strange that day. Well that's why, Marcie's friend was the girl that was in the office that day. I thought if I pretended to be mad at you for forcing me to go to the office, when Marcie heard about it, she wouldn't be angry with me. But I was wrong."

"Why do you think Marcie had anything to do with your being pushed?" Angel questioned.

"Because, when I turned around to see who was running up on me, I got a good look at one of the girls."

"And," Angel prompted.

"And...it was one of the girls with Marcie. They were hanging out in the locker corridor before I left campus that day. "

"So, you saw her with Marcie. That doesn't mean anything."

"There's more. She was more than just with Marcie."

"Okay, so tell me."

"She and Marcie were in the locker corridor when I went with my friends to get my books. Marcie and this other girl were standing close to my locker. I politely asked them to move. At first, they ignored me. Like they didn't hear me, so I raised my voice. That got their attention and that of some of the other kids in the corridor. I guess they didn't want to attract any more attention because Marcie told her to be quiet, she would have an opportunity to deal with me later.

That seemed to satisfy her because she gave me a hard look and moved away. She whispered something to the girl next to her and they burst out laughing. The usual stuff. I got my books and was turning to pass when the other girl standing with Marcie stepped out and bumped me real hard. I would have fallen if Sarah wasn't walking beside me."

"Did you say anything?"

"What was there to say?" She said excuse me like it was an accident or something. I didn't want any trouble, so I let it go."

"What did Marcie do?" Angel asked.

"Nothing," Taylor responded remembering. "She gave me a kinda weird smile and looked away. More like... you know that look you get when you eat something bad. And, she turned away really quick, like she didn't want me to see her face. Now that I think about it, it was a strange thing to do but with Marcie, well strange is her norm."

"You know Taylor," Angel replied, "Ms. Foster told us girls that the police would be getting involved. Seems the girls that pushed you are in a lot of trouble."

"I know they are," Taylor said sighing loudly. "I've already talked with the police."

"What," Angel gasped eyes wide in surprise.

"Yeah, my Mom didn't give me a choice. She said this was way past 'girls being girls' and she wanted it stopped! She then called the police and met them up here to take my statement."

"Your statement," Angel repeated.

"Yeah, sounds like something from one of those criminal shows on television, doesn't it? That's not all. As soon as I'm out of here, we're going to the school to talk with Ms. Mallard. Can you believe my mom is threatening to report Ms. Mallard to the School Superintendent for not doing something about this sooner?"

Taylor cradled her head in her thickly bandaged hands and began to weep.

"This is all my fault," she moaned. "I can't go back there. It was hard enough before but now… All the kids will stare at me. I'll be the laughingstock of the school. And worst of all, I'll be labeled a snitch. It was bad enough being called a traitor, but a snitch. I can't take it. What am I going to do?"

Angel stared at Taylor, feeling her anger rising.

"Excuse me Taylor!" Angel exclaimed her voice sounding rather hard. "What do you mean all your fault? Seems to me there are more people involved in this mess besides you. Yes, you are responsible for your part. But EVERYTHING? Come on. Give me a break. When did you become God?"

Taylor's sobs were abruptly cut off. Lifting her head, she stared open mouthed at Angel.

"What… what?" she stammered, "how am I acting like God?"

"With your Me, Me, Me, attitude! What makes you think you could control everything and take responsibility for everybody's actions? Even God doesn't do that… even though He can. He allows us to make our own decisions, good or bad. He doesn't *make* us.

You, Marcie, and the rest of the girls involved in this mess were given the opportunity to make good choices. But you all chose wrong choices. Choices that didn't make things better but actually made things worse.

Do you even realize, God sent you help—me?" Angel pointed to herself, and my friends. We were all willing to support you and stand with you if you decided to report Marcie and her group to Ms. Mallard. And you put us off. And now here you are beat up and looking a hot mess talking about *this is all my fault!?*" Angel whined mimicking Taylor.

"Well, Taylor, let me tell you something, I'm so through with you. I'm tired of trying to help somebody, no not somebody let me be very clear, YOU. I'm tired of trying to help you when you don't want my help. So, here take this, Angel shoved the devotional into Taylor's hand. "When you finally get off your throne and decide to ask for help, because girl, you really need help, you can come find me?" And with that, Angel turned abruptly and walked out of the hospital room leaving Taylor to stare after her.

* * *

"Wasn't that Angel, your peer mentor?" Mrs. Williams asked entering Taylor's room.

"Yes," Taylor answered still staring at the empty doorway as her mother entered. She could not believe Angel walked out on her like that. Absently, she turned the devotional in her hands.

"Did you hear me?" her mother inquired.

"Ah, what," I'm sorry Mom, my mind was on something else. What did you say?"

"I was asking you what is that?" her Mother questioned, pointing at the small book in Taylor's hand.

"Oh, this…it's a devotional, at least that's what Angel called it."

"Devotional, may I see it?"

"Sure," why not?

Mrs. Williams took the book from Taylor opening it to the page Angel marked. Slowly she began to read.

"Have you read this?" Mrs. Williams asked.

"No, Angel gave it to me, told me to read it and walked out" Taylor answered still puzzled by Angel's strong words.

"You should read it," Mrs. Williams encouraged, a smile pulling up the corners of her mouth. Turning, she walked to the window spotting Angel, she watched as she walked away from the hospital.

Angel stood at the bus stop impatiently pacing back and forth. Watching in the direction the bus was to come, she checked her watch. It should be on its way or at least within eyesight. The sooner she put the hospital and her conversation with Taylor behind her the better. Recalling Taylor's words, she began to fume all over again.

"How dare her!" she said out loud.

"How dare whom?" a voice interrupted her thoughts.

"Eeek! You startled me. "Where did you come from?" Angel asked visibly shaken by the unexpected appearance of the older woman with the large black purse and shopping bag.

"I'm sorry child," the woman replied. "I didn't mean to startle you. Didn't you see me sitting over there, she indicated a bench a few feet away. "I remembered you as the girl with the wonderful hair. It's a shame you keep it up like that. It was so beautiful loose and free. But, to finish answering your question, I saw you and decided to come over here and let you keep me company until your bus or mine comes along. You must have a lot on your mind, to have not noticed me?" the older woman continued.

"I guess so," Angel answered, her heartbeat returning to normal. "I left a fri…, someone that I know in the hospital and she really upset me."

"I hope she is alright?

"Oh, she's alright," Angel spoke dismissing the concern in the older woman's voice. "She will probably be released tomorrow."

"That's good news, isn't it?"

"Yeah, of course, it's, well…"

"Well, what child?"

"She still doesn't get it," the words gushed from Angel. "I've tried over and over again to help her…but she doesn't get it."

"What doesn't she get?"

"That she doesn't have to go through this all by herself, she has us."

"Us?"

"Yeah, us, the God Squad!"

"The what Squad?" the older woman asked not understanding.

"I mean, me and my friends. We call ourselves the God Squad."

"I see," the older woman nodded still not understanding.

"It's a long story," Angel explained seeing the perplexed look on the woman's face. "We offered to help her before she got put in the hospital, but she wanted to wait, and well waiting made the situation worse. And, now, instead of being ready to do something, she's up there crying about everything being her fault, and that she should have done this, and if she did or didn't, none of this would have happened."

"Well, I'm tired of sitting around and doing nothing. The longer we wait, the worse this problem at school is going to get. I can't understand for the life of me why she is so afraid. I could understand if they were giants, but it's only a group of girls and they are not big girls, they are her same age." Angel finished with exasperation evident in her voice.

"Reminds me of the ten spies," the older woman chuckled.

"Exactly," Angel exclaimed. "That's why I left my devotional with her. Maybe Joshua and Caleb can convince her to stand up for herself. I'm so through with her."

"You really sound frustrated."

"Frustrated is not the word for what I feel. I am angry."

"Angry, why are you angry?"

"For one, she doesn't have to take it. And, two, she's not alone like I was…," Angel, stopped, slumping onto the bench like a deflated balloon, her energy spent.

"And you, Angel," the older woman with the dark bronze skin and piercing blue eyes asked; "are you still afraid of the giants even though you are not alone?

Surprised by the question, Angel started to respond but finding no answer, remained silent. Dropping her head, she stared down at her hands going over the question in her mind. Was she still afraid? Hadn't she recently admitted to the girls that she had been afraid? Why was she angry with Taylor for admitting that she too was afraid? She squirmed, uncomfortable with her thoughts, remembering her impatience and her harsh words.

In that moment, she realized her anger was not only with Taylor, but herself as well for not standing up for herself. Here it was years later, and she was still dealing with the memories and feelings of shame and anger. Yes, she admitted to herself, she was fighting her own giants.

How could the older woman know about the giants in her life? She lifted her head to ask, but the woman was no longer sitting beside her. Turning, she saw the bus a short distance away, glimpsed the doors close, and heard the wheezing of the engine as it pulled away.

When had the bus arrived? She didn't hear it, nor did she see the older woman get on the bus, but she saw the doors close and heard the bus pull away.

"That's too weird," Angel said, shrugging her shoulders as the bus drove past her. She would have to remember to ask Ms. Foster about this. Turning, she walked back in the direction of the hospital.

Chapter 9

"What do we do about this whole thing with Marcie and Taylor?" Angel asked.

"I don't know about the rest of you," Chris interjected; "but I think this goes way beyond Marcie and Taylor. There might be a lot more of this kind of behavior going on than we even know about."

"Why do we keep talking about this kind of behavior as if it doesn't have a name?" Sadie said. "Let's call it what it is… BULLYING!"

"Okay, okay" Chris laughed holding her hands up in mock defense. "There is a lot more bullying going on at Carver Preparatory then we even know."

"I agree," Mia replied, "and I think it is time that we do something about it!"

"I'm in agreement that we need to do something," Jade weighed in. "What exactly, I'm not sure. The problem seems so big."

"You're right Jade," Eve agreed, "it is a big problem, but we have got to start doing something. It's like my grandmother asked me, "How do you eat an elephant?""

"What?" Jade asked confused. I thought we were talking about bullying; how did we get on eating elephants?"

"Oh, Jade," Sadie laughed, "you are so funny. Eve didn't mean eating real elephants; that's a metaphor.

"A meta what?" Jade asked more confused than ever.

The girls laughed good naturedly at Jade's obvious confusion.

"That's not funny," Jade replied, color infusing her face. You guys know, I don't like being made fun of."

"I'm sorry," Eve apologized. Didn't mean to make it sound like I was making fun of you. It's... well, the elephant thing seemed to be the best way to get my point across."

"And, what point is that?" Jade asked.

"Okay, Jade, let me ask you...if you had to, how would you eat an elephant?"

"Uhmm, well, since an elephant is so big, I guess... I got it, one small bite at a time!"

"Exactly," Eve said. "Same goes for this project. When we look at all that it will take to get it done it looks to be a really big job. But if we break it down into small do-able pieces, we can do it."

"I get it," Jade replied. "So, a metaphor is like a picture?"

"Yeah," something like that, Eve agreed.

"So, can we get back to what Eve was saying before Miss Jade here got confused?" Sadie interjected.

"No need to be mean," Jade shot back at Sadie. "Everybody is not like you. Some of us don't walk around with a pencil stuck behind our ear and reading books all the time. Some of us are simply ordinary people, you know."

"Jade, Sadie," Ms. Foster interrupted, "that is no way to be talking to each other. Remember, we are to respect each other."

"Yeah, but..." Jade defended, Sadie is always talking down to me. Like she is so smart and I'm dumb or something because I didn't know what Eve was talking about."

"No, Jade," Sadie responded, "I didn't mean to sound like I was talking down to you. I... well, your response was so... literal. It was funny to me because well I too for a moment didn't understand what Eve was talking about. Then I realized she did not mean it literally. She was drawing us a picture. Like you said. Anyway, would you please forgive me?" Sadie asked crossing the room and hugging Jade.

Sadie's apology was met with a wide grin and a firm hug from Jade.

"Now," Eve interrupted, "can I finish what I was talking about?"

"Sure," Jade and Sadie spoke in unison their recent disagreement forgotten as quickly as it started.

"Wait a minute," Sadie interrupted looking from one girl to the other; "Maybe we should begin by talking?"

"But what good is talking?" Angel asked.

"Hear me out," Sadie began slowly as the ideas became clearer in her head. "First, we can begin by talking with the students. Get an idea of how much bullying is going on. Next, we could have a general assembly or something that addresses the problem of bullying."

"Great ideas Sadie!" Mia gushed. "We could even have students that have been bullied tell their stories."

"Yeah, and we could form a committee to come up with a... Anti-Bullying Policy, for the school" Eve added.

"Those are all great ideas," Chris said, "but don't you have to have Ms. Mallard's permission before you can have a general assembly?"

"Ugh," they groaned in unison.

"Yeah, and before we can even take our request to Ms. Mallard, we have to go before the student council," Sadie reminded them.

"Wait," Angel said snapping her fingers, "we, meaning the peer mentors can ask our advisor, she turned to Ms. Foster, to go to the peer mentor Coordinator with our concerns and request Ms. Mallard grant us an assembly!"

"Will you do that?" Angel asked turning to Ms. Foster.

Ms. Foster looked from one girl to the other before answering.

"Yes, I will go to the Coordinator but first you will have to go to the student council, and there is something else you must do," she directed her comment to all the girls. "I need an outline of what it is you are proposing, and I will need it by next week."

"Sounds like a giant size job," Mia sighed.

"Yeah," Angel agreed. "Reminds me of the giants I've been dreaming about lately."

"You still have those dreams?" Jade asked.

"Never mind," Angel dismissed Jade's question. "We have way too much to do to be bothered with my dreams about giants."

Chapter 10

"I'm nervous," Taylor admitted as she walked beside Angel with the others following behind as they headed for Ms. Mallard's office.

"Yeah, so am I," Angel admitted. "But we've tried time and again to meet with Ms. Mallard and she still refuses to talk with us. I don't think we will have much trouble getting in to see her now with all the heat that's been put on her since you and your Mom paid her a visit."

Angel couldn't suppress the smile that came to her face at the thought of Ms. Mallard being confronted by not only Mrs. Williams but also Ms. Foster, Mr. Andrews, the peer mentor Coordinator, and Taylor. She could just image the surprised look on Mrs. Stewart's face when they entered the office with Taylor in front announcing they were there to see Ms. Mallard. She wished she could have been a fly on the wall.

"What are you smiling about?" Taylor asked.

"Oh, nothing much," Angel replied. "Just that I would have given just about anything to have seen the look on Mrs. Stewart's face when you all stormed Ms. Mallard's office. I bet she didn't dismiss you this time with that snooty attitude of hers."

"You're about to find out firsthand," Taylor said, stopping short as they arrived at Ms. Mallard's office. "Is everybody ready," she asked, turning to the group assembled behind her.

"We're all ready," Mia confirmed for the group excitement in her voice. "Let's go to work!"

Taylor pushed open the door. Angel entered first, and the other students followed filling the quiet office with chants of: "Stop bullying now," and carrying signs that said the same thing.

"What is all this…?" Ms. Mallard sputtered coming out of her office to see what all the commotion was about.

"You," she said, eyeing Taylor. "And, I should have known, you would be with her," she indicated noticing Angel.

"Ms. Mallard," Angel spoke in her most adult voice, "we're here to present a petition signed by the Student Council requesting permission to have an anti-bullying assembly."

"I have already addressed that matter with Taylor," Ms. Mallard spoke sternly. "Now, you students need to get out of my office and get to class."

"It's lunch time," one of the students in the group replied.

"Well, whatever," Ms. Mallard, said dismissing them. "I want you all out of here or I will have Mrs. Stewart give you all detention slips and notify your parents of your disruptive behavior. Sarah, is that you? I'm surprised that you are a part of this." Mrs. Stewart, she continued casting a disapproving look at first Sarah then her mother, Mrs. Stewart. "You approve of your daughter's radical behavior?"

"Ms. Mallard," Sarah began, stepping forward, not giving her mother a chance to answer. Clearing her throat, she continued. "My Mom has nothing to do with this. In fact, she doesn't even know I've been bullied. I did like so many of the others here, kept quiet and hoped it would pass. But it didn't and well when Taylor got hurt, I was really scared. I kept thinking that could happen to me and there was no one to help me or make it stop."

"Yeah," another member of the group came forward. "I was scared too. But then Angel asked me if I would be willing to come here and meet with you. I made up my mind this morning, that I am so tired of being afraid, so I'm here with all the others."

"Yeah," they raised their voices in unison and again began to chant, "Stop Bullying Now. Stop Bullying Now."

"Girls, girls…" Ms. Mallard shouted to be heard over the chanting. Stop this nonsense. I already told Taylor that I would take care of everything and that is what I plan to do. Now, please leave my office."

The group did not move. Turning to Mrs. Stewart, she ordered, "Give each one of them detention slips for the next two days."

"Ms. Mallard," Sarah spoke again, "I'm here to support Taylor and the others and finally stand up for myself and say; I've had enough. You can give me detention, and Mom," she said facing her mother, "detention is not as bad as what I've been going through since the beginning of this semester."

Returning her attention to Ms. Mallard, she continued; "You say that what happened between Taylor and Marcie is just girls being girls. Well, no disrespect Ms. Mallard, you're way wrong about this. What's been happening to Taylor, me, and the others here is BULLYING!"

"Sarah," Mrs. Stewart came to stand beside her daughter. Placing her hands on her shoulders, she looked directly in her eyes before continuing, "I'm proud of you baby. I didn't know what was going on but when your behavior changed, and you came home that day wearing your lunch, I knew something had happened. I just wish you could have told me, but we'll talk about that later."

Turning to Ms. Mallard, she said; "Now is the time for us to do something about all this. I stand with the girls. It's time we take a stand against bullying and let everyone at Carver Preparatory know that we will not tolerate this type of behavior"

"Yeah," Angel chimed in, "NO More Bullying is our motto!"

Seeing the determination of the students, Ms. Mallard reluctantly agreed to a meeting but not without a few stipulations. First, they needed at least 200 students willing to admit they had been bullied since coming to Carver Prep; and secondly, those in favor of a no bullying policy. If they could get the required information to her by Friday, she would meet with the group representatives.

After the meeting with Ms. Mallard, the girls had announced a meeting would be held the next day at the table under the trees. All those wanting to continue with the project were to bring their lunch and come prepared with ideas and a willingness to work.

Angel gave Ms. Foster an update on their meeting with Ms. Mallard. Things had not gone as they had hoped but Ms. Mallard had not flatly refused to give them a chance. After talking with Ms. Foster, she left the sanctuary anxious to get to the meeting.

"What's this?" Angel asked coming to the table. "Are we the only ones wanting this project to go forth?"

"Well, it looks that way," Mia said. "But you know what they say about looks?"

"I know Jade interjected, "they are deceiving."

"Right," Eve stated, "so I suggest, we pray."

"Let me pray," Sadie volunteered.

"Okay, Sadie, go for it" Eve said.

"Father, thank you that you have given us the opportunity to make real important changes here at Carver Prep. Thing is, we can't do it by ourselves. We need workers. So, we are asking you to send us some workers. We ask this in your Son, Jesus' name. Amen."

"Guys look!" Mia exclaimed.

"Sorry, we're late," Taylor explained coming to the table and bringing with her five others, "but we kind of got held up."

"Held up?" Angel questioned raising her right eyebrow.

"Yeah," Taylor continued explaining, "Sarah here actually got pushed up against her locker in the corridor. If, we didn't come along when we did, no telling what those girls would have done."

"Are you alright Sarah?" Sadie asked.

"I'm, okay," Sarah replied her voice shaky, tears welling in her eyes. "I just hope we can do something about all of this. I don't know how long I can take this treatment." The tears began rolling down her cheeks. "Do you know it's not just at school but now they're getting to me at home? Somehow they got my email and are sending me all kinds of nasty messages threatening me and calling me a snitch."

Sadie placed her arm on Sarah's shoulder allowing her to lean against her as she sobbed out the hurt of her latest encounter with bullies.

"I'm sorry," Sarah sniffed. "I must sound like such a coward to you all, especially after I talked so strongly in front of Ms. Mallard. But, well, it's one thing when I'm with all of you, and another when I'm alone."

"I know," Angel agreed. "That's the way I felt until I met a group of kids that were willing to protect me, so to speak. Thing is, they weren't exactly the right kids to be with. And, I ended up getting into a lot of trouble. Which later led to me meeting up with these girls… the God Squad."

"God Squad?" Sarah questioned.

"God Squad," Mia repeated. "That's what we call ourselves but we're just ordinary girls, like you, living ordinary lives.

"And then," Jade stepped forward taking a warrior stance, "we get the call and we become... The God Squad," they responded in unison.

"Okay, God Squad, or whatever, you call yourselves," Taylor interrupted, "if we plan on meeting Ms. Mallard's stipulations, we better get to work because we have a giant size job ahead of us."

The girls looked at each. Chris winked, shrugged her shoulders and said:

"It's a good thing we know a giant slayer."

Taylor gave the girls a quizzical look, started to speak but thought better of it. Pulling out her notebook, she began sharing with the girls some of her ideas. She was secretly pleased when they readily accepted her idea for the questionnaire about bullying. It was simple, have you been bullied, yes or no? Would you like to see Carver Prep adopt an anti-bullying policy, yes or no?

After, Eve talked with Paul, the President of the Student Council, he allowed them to place a box in the student council office where the questionnaires would be deposited. One of Taylor's fellow art students made a comical sign that indicated where to place the questionnaires.

As impossible as the task before them seemed to be, they followed the suggestions of their counselors and the peer mentor Coordinator and bit-by-bit, step-by-step, they made progress. But they still needed help. Angel shared her concerns with Eve as they walked to class on Wednesday.

"I know somebody that can get us all the help we need,"

Eve said. "I'll see if he's willing to come to our next meeting." "He," Angel said surprised by Eve's answer.

"Yes, he," Eve replied. "Do you want help or not?"

"Of course, but…

"But what?" Eve challenged.

"Nothing," Angel mumbled.

He, Paul Manning, President of the Student Council showed up for the last ten minutes of the meeting. Eve blushed profusely as she introduced him to the group. But, as Eve said, he was able to get them the help they needed.

Thursday morning before classes while students lingered in the Quad talking, Operation No Bullying Petition was in full force. Paul was able to rally students together and with the assistance of Eve, they put together committees in charge of making signs, getting signatures, and assigning stations. Stations were set up in the Quad, near the locker corridor, outside the cafeteria, and library. Some students walked around with a clipboard and obtained signatures, and some teachers that supported the students' effort, allowed announcements to be made in their class.

Friday afternoon came all too quickly but before Paul and Eve left the Student Council Office a preliminary count of the petitions showed good results. Angel and Taylor stayed behind to finish counting the questionnaires and signatures of the few remaining ballots. Angel looked up hearing someone enter the office.

"Hey Marcie," she greeted trying to hide the surprise in her voice.

Hearing Marcie's name, Taylor's head shot up.

"What's wrong, cat got your tongue?" Marcie asked.

"No, you surprised me that's all," Taylor answered.

"Yeah, well," Marcie shrugged appearing nonchalant. "Wanted to turn my questionnaire in but seeing you're finished counting them, I guess I'm too late." Turning, she made to walk away.

"Hold on," Angel stopped her. "We're not finished, we have a whole stack of questionnaires over here left to count. Give me yours and I'll put it in the middle of the stack that way Taylor, nor I, will know what you answered."

"Thanks, I appreciate that, but it's not necessary. I'll tell you. Have I been bullied...?," giving first Angel and then Taylor, a long look, she replied... "YES. Would I like to see Carver Prep start a no-bulling program? The answer is again...YES." Turning, she walked out of the room leaving Taylor and Angel staring after her.

***

Angel desperately pulled against the ropes restraining her. Her struggles seeming to cause the bands to hold her tighter.

"Stop struggling," Eve shouted over the giant's booming laughter and loud thudding of his feet as he made his way to Angel.

"Help me, somebody please help me?" Angel screamed, as the giant drew closer the earth shaking with each step of his gigantic feet. But the more she struggled, the tighter the ropes became.

"Angel, Angel," Chris shouted, "Stop struggling. Just stand up?"

"I can't," Angel replied, screwing her neck around to see Eve carrying the Shield of Faith hoisted in front of her, deflecting the fiery arrows hurled by the giant. Chris stood near Eve, arms upheld, wearing the Breastplate of Righteousness. Each lightning bolt sent toward Angel, was deflected by the Breastplate sending a blinding flash back to the giant causing him to stumble backwards.

"Yes, you can," came the voice of Mia, taking her warrior stance, her sharp two-edged sword swishing through the blanket of darkness hurled her way.

"Angel," Jade shouted as the vibration of truth and love emitted from the Helmet of Salvation disintegrated the clawing fingers of fear and hate drifting toward Angel. "Just stand up and be still," she commanded her voice full of authority.

"I'm here with the others," Sadie called from Angel's left. "Don't listen to the giants," Sadie directed. Whipping off the Belt of Truth she began zapping the lies fired like lightning bolts from the giant filling the space between her and Angel.

"I'm scared," Angel screeched in anguish. "They are too big for me to handle."

"Don't be afraid," Chris called out over the roaring laughter of the giant. "Guard your heart Angel! Just stand up!"

Angel tiring from her desperate struggle looked up. Frightened, her heart beating wildly the giant now stood in front of her, his club raised high above his head a grotesque smile exposing his rotten and missing teeth. The stench of lies and deception caused Angel to gag.

With all her remaining strength, she pushed her back firmly against the pole. Her legs trembled with her efforts and gave way. Praying for strength, she again strained to stand. "Eeeek," she screeched, closing her eyes in fear as the giant's club came down only inches from her causing the ground to shake. Throwing his head back the giant let out a loud mocking laugh his foul breath causing Angel to swoon.

"Stand up, hah," the giant mocked. "You can't stand up. I'm too strong for you and your little friends. Your weapons are no match for me," he laughed beating his fist against his chest.

"Angel open your eyes," Jade screamed jumping into action. "Remember, the Helmet of Salvation! It will guard your mind. Stop looking at the size of the giant! Look up! Look at God! He's greater and stronger than anything that can come against you!!! Stand up and stand still. We're all here. He can't harm you."

"Stand up Angel!" the girls yelled in unison.

Angel closed her eyes tightly, tears streaming down her cheeks, heart pounding. With one final push, she strained to stand. She did it! Suddenly, the ropes holding her began to loosen and fall away. Amazed, Angel opened her eyes seeing the ropes indeed were falling from her. Freeing her hands, she pushed free of the ropes from around her. Stepping away from them, she gained her footing. Looking down at her feet, she saw the Shoes of Peace. Stomping first her right foot and then her left. She stood tall, back straight, feet secure in the Shoes of Peace, firmly planted on the ground. Slowly, she raised her head eyes meeting the menacing glare of the giant looming over her.

Crossing her arms across her chest and with a boldness she did not know she possessed, she spoke to the giant.

"You might be too strong for me, but you are no match for the One that lives in me!"

"Yeah," Sadie said coming alongside Angel, whipping the Belt of Truth, toward the giant catching him around the neck. "Your lies can no longer rule here." The giant coughed, a black mist spewing from his mouth as the Belt of Truth tightened around his neck. Dropping his club, he clutched hopelessly trying to loosen the belt from his neck.

"Oh, no you don't," Mia said, moving quickly in front of the giant. With the Sword of the Spirit held high, leaping toward the giant, in mid-air gave a mighty swing. Swoosh! She delivered a fatal blow to the head of the giant. Eve rushed to the group covering them with the Shield of Faith as the giant off balance

began stumbling all the while spewing a barrage of fiery darts at the girls. As the giant staggered toward Angel, she stuck out her foot effectively tripping him. With a loud thud, he fell to the ground.

The girls stood quietly looking on the giant. Now, he didn't seem so large. Thunder rumbled overhead followed closely by streaks of lightening flashing across the sky before the rain began to fall, first a few drops then a downpour. The girls huddled together watching in amazement as the rain falling on the giant reduced him to steam that slowly evaporated into the air. As quickly as the storm came, so it passed. The clouds rolled away exposing a beautiful blue sky the sun heralding a bright sunny day!

Angel looked from one girl to the other. She stretched her right hand, taking the hand of Chris with her left she took the hand of Sadie; the others joined hands. A knowing look passed between them, each knowing they could not have fought and won this battle without the other. Silently, they came together hugging tightly. When they looked out over the campus where once darkness and chaos had reigned, now the brightness of a new day was punctuated by the sound of the student's laughter as they made their way through the corridors.

"They're gone," Angel exclaimed sitting up in bed. They're all gone!

"Who's gone?" Amber asked standing near Angel's bed.

"The… never mind," Angel said, shaking the dream from her mind.

"You've had one of those dreams again," Amber stated.

"No," Angel, scrambling from her bed a smile on her face. "This was definitely not one of those dreams, Amber. In fact," she stopped, turning to face Amber before heading for the bathroom, "they're gone, they are all GONE!"

Chapter 11

"Ms. Mallard, Angel and Taylor are here to see you," Mrs. Stewart announced.

"Ugh, Ms. Mallard grunted, "I was hoping they would just give up, but I guess I underestimated them. All of this commotion about bullying. Carver Preparatory School doesn't have a bullying problem, what it has is over-zealous peer mentors. The worst thing that could happen to any school—peer mentors," she mumbled, "that's why I'm cutting the program from the budget next year."

"Cutting what?" Mrs. Stewart asked.

"Nothing, nothing," Ms. Mallard replied, waving Mrs. Steward away. "I'm busy."

"But what about the students? Do you want me to send them in?"

"No, no, of course not! Give me half hour or so. I want to get this report finished for the School Superintendent before I meet with them."

"But that report isn't due until…"

"I know when it's due," Ms. Mallard spoke sharply the irritation evident in her voice. "Now, if you will excuse me, I want to get back to work. I will tell you when I'm ready to meet with those students. Go and close the door behind you."

Mrs. Stewart went back to the group of eager students assembled in the office. Cringing inwardly, she chose her words carefully.

"I'm sorry… Ms. Mallard has a… very important report she is working on and asks that you wait, and she will see you as soon as she can."

"Did she say how soon, as soon as possible would be?" Angel asked, a funny feeling starting in her stomach.

"She said a half hour or more," Mrs. Stewart replied.

"I can't stay that long," one of the girls in the group announced.

"Me neither," said another one.

Angel looked at the group.

"Go if you have to. Is there anyone else that needs to go?" Angel asked surprised by the number of hands that went up. "That many. Okay, then go!"

The girls quickly left the office, leaving Angel, Taylor, Mia, Sadie, Jade, Chris and Taylor's three friends, Sarah, Amy, and Rebecca.

"What happened to Eve?" Angel asked to no one in particular.

Thirty minutes passed, then forty-five. Mrs. Stewart began gathering her things preparing to leave. The intercom buzzed. After a terse exchange of words, Mrs. Stewart hung up the phone and turned to the group.

"Ms. Mallard apologizes for the delay. She wants to know if she can re-schedule the meeting to a more convenient time."

"More convenient?" Angel asked the irritation evident in her voice. "Convenient for whom, certainly not us. We held to our end of the agreement and now she is going back on her end!"

"Angel, calm down," Chris tried soothing Angel. "We can meet another time, it's okay."

"No!" Angel said, "it is not okay. We worked hard to get the information she wanted and now, she won't meet with us because she has to get out a report."

"I'm sorry," Mrs. Stewart apologized. "Do you want me to take those papers and give them to Ms. Mallard?"

"No," Angel replied, "I'll keep them for a more convenient time."

"I knew it," Taylor said slumping against the wall outside Ms. Mallard's office.

"Knew what?" Angel asked.

"That you can't go up against giants and expect to win."

"What?" Angel asked as it became clear what Taylor was saying.

"Look at what happened," Taylor continued. "We did everything we could, but well it wasn't enough."

"Taylor," Angel spoke louder than she intended. Taking a deep breath, she lowered her voice, reminding herself to stop, wait before speaking.

"What?" Taylor answered, when Angel did not continue right away.

"Do you think that this is over?" Angel asked.

"Remember, the devotion?"

"Well, yeah, but if Ms. Mallard won't meet with us, what can we do?

"Haven't you learned anything from hanging around with us? We're the God Squad remember. And, yes, things look pretty impossible right now, but we are not on a mission impossible, we're on a Mission Him-Possible."

"What is a Mission Him-Possible?" Taylor asked looking from one girl to the next.

"It's a 'with God all things are possible mission,'" Chris explained. "We've done all we can so now, the rest is up to Him. We have to have faith that this will work out for our good!"

"I don't know," Taylor hedged. You guys are always talking about God and praying about stuff, but I don't understand. How can you still have hope? Looks like to me this is over.

"Yeah, I know," Mia agreed but, remember that devotional Angel gave you. You know about the two different reports the spies brought back. One was impossible, and the other was Him possible. Well, that's what this is. I know it looks hopeless and we're coming up against some giant obstacles, but remember…"

"I know," Taylor interjected, "we have the giant slayer on our side."

"You got it!" Angel exclaimed. "You really got it!"

"So now," Mia added, "we just step back and let God do His thing!"

"That's a strange way to put it," Taylor laughed, "but it makes sense. So, I'll just go along with you guys. Anyway, I want to see how God handles Ms. Mallard."

They all burst out laughing as each thought of the numerous ways God could deal with Ms. Mallard.

"What's so funny?" Eve asked joining the group.

"It's a long story," Angel replied, giving Eve a hard look. "We'll catch you up later. Right now, it's back to the drawing board." And, with that, she turned abruptly walking away from the group.

* * *

"Does anyone know why Ms. Foster called this meeting?" Mia asked the other members of the God Squad.

"I don't. Thought maybe one of you would know;" Sadie answered.

"I'm sure we'll find out soon enough," Jade replied. "By the way, anyone seen Eve and Angel?"

"They're here," Chris answered. "They are in the back, with Ms. Foster."

"The Reckoning Room?" Jade asked turning a concerned look in the direction of the back room. "Is everything alright?" They knew the back room was reserved by Ms. Foster whenever she needed to have a "discussion" with one or more of the girls.

"Wow, this must be serious," Mia added.

"Why don't we just wait and see?" Chris said stopping any further comments from Mia.

A short time later Ms. Foster followed by Eve and Angel emerged from the back room.

"Good afternoon, girls," Ms. Foster greeted coming into the room. "I'm so glad you were all able to come at such short notice but something important has come up and we need to talk about it.

"What's it about?" Mia inquired, her eyes darting from Eve and then Angel as they came into the circle.

"You'll find out soon enough," Ms. Foster answered. "First, who wants to pray?"

"I do," Chris volunteered. "Father thank you for this mission that we are on. Thank you for all that you have done thus far, the people we have met, friends and foes. It's challenging Father, but we know we can do it, because You said we can with Your help. I pray for my friends here in this circle. Help us to remember we love each other but most of all help us to remember, You love us."

The girls looked from Angel then to Eve. Angel and Eve were the two oldest members of the God Squad and the girls looked up to them. For them to have been called to the "reckoning room" signaled something serious was afloat.

Ms. Foster brought the meeting to order. "Alright girls, I understand you did not meet with Ms. Mallard as planned. Angel has given me an update. Is there anything else anyone wants to add?"

"I do," Mia spoke up. "We went in there all prepared, a whole group of us. We had all the signatures Ms. Mallard required plus some. In fact, just about the whole school agreed we have a bullying prob… excuse me a bullying challenge," Mia corrected seeing the raised eyebrow of Ms. Foster.

"Yeah," Sadie jumped in. "We were all ready to give her our petition and all and she didn't even come out and see us. Had her secretary tell us she had to complete a report for the Superintendent."

"Did she re-schedule?" Ms. Foster asked.

"No," Chris answered, "She said she would get back to us at a quote 'more convenient time.'"

"And," Ms. Foster prompted.

"And, nothing," Angel spoke up. "Just like I told you, that was a week ago, and she still hasn't met with us."

"So," Ms. Foster asked, "what are your plans?"

The girls looked from one to the other. Finally, Jade spoke.

"Well, we really haven't talked about anything… since, well, since that meeting."

"And why is that?" Ms. Foster asked.

"Um, An…, I mean, we, haven't gotten together."

"Don't you meet for lunch every day?" Ms. Foster asked.

"Well, usually, we do," Mia answered, "but…" her voice trailed off, her eyes darting from Angel to Eve.

"It's alright guys," Eve intervened. Turning to Ms. Foster, she explained. "They're trying to cover for me and Angel's bad behavior this past week. As, I told you in our meeting, Angel and I have not been talking with each other since the meeting in Ms. Mallard's office. So, I guess that's why she hasn't been coming to the spot."

"So, you, nor the group don't know why?" Ms. Foster directed her question to the group.

The girls looked at each other, then back at Ms. Foster, each hunching their shoulders.

"What does this mean?" Ms. Foster asked, hunching her shoulders.

"It means, we don't know," Sadie answered.

"Don't you think we need to know?" The girls nodded their agreement to Ms. Foster's question. "Good then," she continued. "Angel, do you want to tell the group why you haven't been meeting with them?"

Angel hesitated, clearing her throat. "It's like Eve said, I was angry with her and didn't want to talk or be around her. I know that wasn't fair to the rest of you," Angel explained looking from one girl to the next, "but at the time, I was only thinking about myself."

Ms. Foster's question broke the silence that followed Angel's response.

"Does anyone have anything they want to say to Angel?"

"Yeah, I do," Chris said, the frustration evident in her voice. "Angel, you keep forgetting, you are not in this alone. We are a TEAM, remember? You didn't have to stop coming to our spot just because you were angry with Eve. We could have talked it out. But you didn't give us a chance."

"I know that now, now that I'm not so emotional but at the time, well…," Angel finished shrugging her shoulders.

Again, the group went silent. All eyes focused on Angel. Eve broke the silence.

"Guys, it's okay," she assured them. "Angel and I have talked it out and, we're good. I knew how important that meeting was but, well… I got so busy with what I was doing, I lost track of time. She had a right to be upset with me. She's here now and that's what's important. I think we should give her a pass on this one."

"I don't know," Chris said, a twinkle in her eye. "We've been giving our girl here a lot of passes lately, maybe we need to come up with something else… like maybe a time-out?"

"Time-out?" Angel repeated. "I'm too…."

"Too what?" Sadie asked.

Angel dropped her head, color infusing her cheeks.

"I was going to say grown up then I thought about my behavior and, well, I haven't been acting very grown up lately, have I?

"No, you haven't!" Mia responded. "So, guys, she said including the others in the group. Instead of a time-out why don't we do this...," she paused for emphasis. "Every time, Angel gets angry, we all surround her and give her puppy dog kisses on her cheeks until she isn't angry anymore?"

"What?" the girls asked in unison.

"Yeah," Mia continued. "It will give Angel time to cool off and maybe then she can think straight. It's better than putting her on time-out."

"Oh, come on guys," Angel protested. "Give me a break. I'm not that bad!"

"According to you, maybe," Sadie responded, "but we're the ones that have been dealing with your, how do I put this, *ugly attitude* lately."

"Yeah," Jade agreed. "You've been pretty difficult to get along with lately. Seriously, it's taken a lot of prayer to keep us quiet."

"Anyone, else feel like that?" Angel asked surveying the girls around her.

"Well," since you're asking, Chris replied. "I think you've been acting about as bad as you did when you first came to the group. I was hoping, no praying it would pass especially after the talk we had but seems you're still having a difficult time and still reacting the same way. And, now this thing with Eve. I was shocked especially the way you acted in front of Taylor and all."

"I... I... know that was... bad on my part, but, well... I was angry. First Ms. Mallard stood us up, after all our hard work, and then Eve showed up late and... I just blew."

"We know," Mia exclaimed. "How, well we know. A blind man could see that."

"You know, Mia," Angel retorted feeling uncomfortable with the comments about her, "you don't have to be so sarcastic. I get the point."

"Alright, girls," Ms. Foster intervened. "I think you have all made it quite clear how you feel about Angel's past behavior. And, Angel," she said directing her gaze at Angel. "I think you realize that your behavior over the past two weeks has not been in line with that of a Peer Mentor or a member of the God Squad."

"No…, it hasn't," Angel replied. "That's why, I'm thinking of leaving the group."

"Leaving!" Mia repeated. "How are you going to leave the group? Ms. Foster, can she do that?"

"If that is her choice," Ms. Foster explained, "then we have to respect that choice whether we like it or not."

"But, but she can't leave," Mia wailed. "We are the God Squad and the God Squad can't go into battle without the Shoes of the Gospel of Peace. We'll get all off balance and stuff."

"That's right," Jade spoke up. "You can't leave, Angel. We need you."

"I appreciate you saying that," Angel replied, "but seems to me, you don't need me with my bad attitude."

"You're right, we don't, need your bad attitude," Chris answered, "but we need you. That is, the you that is not hurting so badly you keep striking out at the ones that are closest to you."

"Yeah, Angel," Eve said, coming to sit next to Angel placing her arm across her shoulder and pulling her close. "We need you."

"Are you sure?" Angel asked looking sheepishly from one girl to the next.

"We're sure," Mia said taking the seat on the other side of Angel. "And to show you how sure we are...," she began planting puppy dog kisses on Angel's cheek.

"Ewww, get off of me," Angel protested as the other girls joined in kissing Angel.

Later that night as Angel lay in her bed, she found her mind too filled with thoughts from the meeting to allow her to fall asleep. After tossing and turning, punching her pillow and readjusting the covers on her bed, she flopped over on her back staring up at the ceiling giving in to her thoughts.

The girls were right, she admitted. She had been acting very... what was it Sadie had said she had: an *ugly attitude*. That comment had really hit hard. She knew she had a temper, but it had been a long time since she had expressed it to anyone outside of her family. Usually, her younger sister Amanda had been the recipient of her anger. But that was changing. Lately, she found herself getting angry more and more.

She hated the way she felt when she got angry... like something took control of her. Afterwards, she would feel sorry and ashamed wanting only to run away. Angel cringed inwardly at the thought that she would leave the God Squad because she could not handle her temper.

She admitted to herself, she needed help. She could no longer overlook or dismiss her bursts of anger. Deciding to call Ms. Foster first thing in the morning, she slowly drifted off to sleep thinking about the just in case clause.

Chapter 12

Angel and Taylor walked through the locker corridor stopping at Taylor's locker long enough for her to stash her book and retrieve her lunch. As they exited the corridor, the large anti-bullying sign came into view. Sharing a knowing look, they burst into girlish laughter as they headed to the spot to meet up with the other girls.

"What are you two so happy about?" Mia asked as the girls approached.

"That!" Taylor answered pointing to the large anti-bullying sign posted on the tree. "We did it, she squealed delightedly. "We got an anti-bullying policy at Carver Preparatory Academy!"

"Yes, we did," Angel said. "And, to think, you doubted that we would."

"I know," Taylor replied. "At first, I thought it was impossible, but now I know it was Him-Possible!"

"Listen to you. I think we have made a believer of you," Chris said.

"Well, maybe not all the way," Taylor answered, "but, I definitely know that with God's help and guidance, you can become a giant slayer!"

"Glad we could be of service," Jade replied.

"No, seriously," Taylor continued, "I could not have gotten through this mess or had the courage to stand up and say no more bullying. I don't like it and I'm not being silent anymore!"

"That took a lot of courage," Angel said. "Especially, when the police got involved. I would have been scared too."

"Well," Taylor admitted. "It wasn't because I was so brave when I had to tell the police about Marcie and those other girls threatening me. That had more to do with my mother. She wouldn't let me do anything else. And, I'm glad she forced me to confront those girls."

"Yeah, I heard Marcie got expelled and has to do something like 1,000 hours community service for her part in the whole thing," Angel said. "But what happened to the other two?"

"They were charged with assault." Taylor supplied.

"Wow," Mia interjected. "That sounds serious."

"It is," Taylor answered. "From what I was told, they will be going to a youth detention facility for six months. After that, they will also have to complete 1,000 hours of community service."

The girls sat quietly taking in what Taylor shared with them. Marcie, and her friends were paying a high price for what Ms. Mallard had termed *girls being girls.*

"No," Taylor broke the silence. "I couldn't have got through this without all of you."

"It wasn't just us," Angel reminded the group. "It took everyone getting involved – students, teachers, and administrators. We all had a hand in this."

"Yeah," Taylor said, "I thought all you guys were going to do was pray about the matter but then… well, you showed me. You put action to your prayers and when you did all you could then you stepped back and… like Mia said, let God do His thing!"

"I know," Mia exclaimed, "and wow He sure did take care of Ms. Mallard. I feel sorry for her."

"Sorry," Taylor echoed. "I think she got off easy. To think, she was trying to get rid of the peer mentoring Program. If it hadn't been for the program, I mean a peer mentor, she said looking at Angel, I would never have told anyone about being bullied."

"I think I understand what you mean," Jade said. "It's not that you're sorry, she had to leave Caver Prep but just that it was too bad that she… couldn't see the real problem."

"Yeah," Sadie added, "it was like she was blaming the peer mentors for bringing the problem to her attention like they started the whole thing. I'm glad Ms. Foster and the peer mentor Coordinator went to her with not only the peer mentor's concerns but those of the students too."

"I know," Taylor agreed. "If they hadn't intervened, the whole thing would have been lost. I don't have to remind you all, I was ready to just give up."

"You weren't the only one." Angel said, "Things looked awfully bad for a while. Seriously, looked like the giants were going to win, but… we hung in there! And, we cut them down one by one!"

The girls were so engrossed in their conversation, they did not become aware of Sarah until she spoke.

"Hi, guys," Sarah greeted the group. "Um, do you mind if I join you?"

"Sure, come on, you can sit by me," Mia said making space for her.

"Hey Sarah," Chris spoke. "Surprised to see you here."

"I know, but, well there is something, I needed to tell all of you, including Taylor," Sarah began, "and I knew I would find you all out here."

"So, tell us already," Mia said.

"First, I want to thank you all for your help and support. You have no idea, well you might, but I was so afraid. I've never been that scared in my life. But... anyway, you know the story, so thanks to all of you. I thought, it was only me and Taylor but when those other students shared their stories, well it gave me courage."

"We appreciate the thanks," Angel replied, "but as we were just saying, it took all of us, you included."

"That's good of you to say," Sarah said, "but...well, I didn't feel like I was doing enough. I kept thinking I needed to do more, which brings me to my next point. That is... the Superintendent recommended me to serve on the Mayor's Anti-Bullying Task Force as their student representative. We're charged with implementing anti-bullying polices throughout all the city schools."

"Wow! Congratulations," they chorused.

"The Superintendent couldn't have made a better choice," Taylor added.

"I agree!" Chris said. "Girl, your research really opened our eyes. Who knew bullying was such a big problem in our schools?

"Chris, weren't you doing some research on bullying?" Sadie asked.

"Yes, but well I had just scratched the surface," Chris replied. "Sarah actually did a more in-depth study of the problem. All that information was helpful in writing the anti-bullying policy."

"Yeah, and, let us not forget the standing ovation Sarah received from the student body when she gave her speech!" Sadie reminded them.

"Thanks guys," Sarah blushed. "My knees were knocking the whole time I was speaking. I'm just glad my voice wasn't shaking."

"No one could tell you were nervous," Chris said. "You handled the whole thing like a pro, especially, when you read that report to the school board on the number of bullying incidences reported to Principal Mallard. The whole room went silent when you said only three had been addressed."

"Oh, by the way, did anyone beside me see the look on Ms. Mallard's face when the chair of the school board informed her that if she was not able to implement the policy as written, they would have to get someone that could," Mia interjected.

"You would bring that up," Sadie said. "But just to let you all know, even Ms. Mallard got some good out of this. I heard, she has left the charter school system and is an administrator for adult education."

"Okay," Mia replied. "So, even Ms. Mallard got something good of this. Enough about her, let's get back to what Sarah was saying."

"I just wanted to ask Taylor are you sure you're okay with me filling the position? I know you were also being considered, and, well, I just wanted to make sure you are alright with it."

"Don't be silly," Taylor answered, "we both know, you are the best choice. I'm happy for you! And besides," she said pointing to the poster on the tree, "my anti-bullying posters will be placed in all schools adopting the city Anti-Bullying policy."

"That's great Taylor," Angel replied. "We're happy for you."

"Happy about what?" Eve asked joining the group.

Everyone fell silent as they looked from Angel to Eve and back to Angel remembering the last time Eve showed up late.

Angel took a deep breath, before speaking.

"We were congratulating Sarah here on being selected as the student representative to serve on the Mayor's Anti-Bullying Task Force."

Eve's big smile showed her appreciation to Angel. The girls let out a collective sigh. Eve looked from Angel to Sarah,

"Well, congratulations, Sarah. I know you will do an excellent job."

"Thank you all," Sarah repeated, "now I have to go to the library, I have some research to do. This whole bullying thing is a lot more common than I thought."

"Wait up," Taylor said, "I'll go with you. See you girls around."

"Angel," Mia spoke as soon as Sarah and Taylor were out of hearing distance, "what's up with you?"

"What do you mean?" Angel asked feigning innocence.

"Yeah," Jade asked, "who are you and where is Angel?"

"I know, I know," Mia answered. "It was those puppy dog kisses we gave her."

"I will punch the first one of you that tries that again," Angel warned. "If you must know, I've been praying and working on my issues with Ms. Foster and I've got a little technique that really helps me."

"Come on Angel," Jade pleaded, "tell us your technique."

"Okay, okay. Whenever, I think about anger, I see red right. Well red reminds me of fire. So, what puts out a fire? Water. So instead of counting to ten, I repeat stop, wait, and then I imagine a huge gush of water pouring from the sky putting out the fire. Works every time."

"Water? That's your technique?" Jade echoed.

"I don't care what it is," Eve replied. "Whatever you're doing, please keep on doing it."

"You know what would be nice," Mia said changing the conversation, "a root beer float. Do I have any takers?"

One by one the girls agreed to meet for root beer floats after school.

Epilogue

"Calling all girls; calling all girls," the call went out notifying the girls there was a meeting at the Sanctuary. Each girl made her way to the meeting place. A lot had happened since they began this mission and they were eager to bring it to a close.

"Well ladies," Ms. Foster spoke entering the room and calling the meeting to order. Settling herself in the high-backed rattan chair, she continued.

"Congratulations on another successful Mission Him-Possible."

"I guess you could call it that," Angel spoke up first, eyeing the other members of the group assembled in the circle.

"What do you mean, you guess?" Mia asked. "We did exactly what we needed to do. We helped a fellow student and got an anti-bullying policy established at Carver Preparatory."

"Yeah," Jade exclaimed; "and if that wasn't enough, we no longer have to deal with Principal Mallard! Who by the way has a position more suitable for her... shall I say *academic qualifications*.

"That's a nice way of putting it!" Mia returned.

"You know Angel, Mia and Jade are right," Eve spoke. "I'd say, we had a very successful mission."

"It's not that," Angel, hesitated, cleared her throat and started again. "It's just well, this mission was really hard. It brought up a lot of things for me and put me at odds with all of you. Turning to Eve, she continued; especially you Eve. I feel so awful about how I acted and…all the terrible things I said to you. I don't know how you can stand to be in the same room with me, yet alone talk to me. I know I've apologized before, but I just want to ask you to forgive me."

"I already did," Eve replied. "Angel, don't you know that your bad attitude and quick temper cannot stop me from loving you. Girl, you are my girl! You have been since the first day we met. Even though you looked like a tough girl with all that dark make-up around your eyes, black outlined, red lips, torn t-shirt, and chewing gum like there was no tomorrow…!"

"Don't forget about her rolling her eyes at everything that was said!" Chris interrupted.

"Oh, yeah, and that too," Eve laughed. "I saw through you then and I saw through you during this whole mission. You're not as tough as you make out to be and I know that. Just like when you joined our group. You were scared. Same holds for this mission, you were scared and didn't want any of us to know, so you do what you do, play tough girl."

Angel dropped her head momentarily, then looked directly into Eve's eyes.

"You're right," she admitted. "I was scared, like I said before but after a while, I gained some confidence because all of you were there for me. But there was something else that scared me…"

When Angel did not continue, Chris prompted her;

"And, what was that Angel?" I thought you got rid of the giants."

"So, did I, until Eve showed up late for our protest in Ms. Mallard's office with that, that…boy."

"Angel!" Eve exclaimed, "don't tell me you were jealous."

"No, not jealous," Angel continued. "I was scared. Scared, I was losing my friend. And, well, I got angry."

"So, that's what all the attitude was about, you thinking I was no longer going to be your friend?"

Angel could only nod her head.

"Why didn't you say something? Even when Ms. Foster had that meeting with us, you didn't say anything. No, I take that back, you said a lot, but you never mentioned "that boy." Oh, by the way, his name is Paul."

How could I? I felt so silly. And, anyway, I didn't really understand what I was feeling until I talked with Ms. Foster. She helped me understand about my "fear."

"Fear?"

"Yeah, fear. F-E-A-R. False emotions appearing real.

The girls sat quietly listening as Angel continued.

"You see when I was bullied all those years ago, the fear of being alone took hold of me. I never wanted to be alone because being alone meant I was vul-ner-able, I think that's the word, right Ms. Foster. Ms. Foster nodded her head in acknowledgment and Angel continued.

"Anyway, you all know how serious I am and that I get angry really quick. Well, I learned during this mission, that anger wasn't the only giant in my life. I don't understand it all, but I do know that when I saw Eve with, that boy... Paul, I got angry. So angry I didn't want to talk to her or be around her. I didn't realize how much pain I was in until I started talking with Ms. Foster. She helped me to see that I used anger to mask my fear. Fear that Eve wouldn't remain my friend.

I didn't think Eve could be my friend, all our friend, she indicated the girls sitting in the circle and a member of the God Squad and hang out with Paul! I didn't understand why she needed to bring someone else into our circle. I thought because she was hanging out with Paul, things would change for us. Like maybe she wouldn't be available to go with us to the diner and maybe even worse she wouldn't have time for us."

"Sounds, like instead of us, you mean you," Chris observed.

"I guess, well, yes, me," Angel admitted.

"Wow Angel!" Eve said. "You really were going through a lot. I thought it was something simple like, maybe a bad period, you know PMS but all this… its heavy"

"Yeah, I know," Angel replied. "Fear is a terrible thing. I understand now why the Bible says, "it causes torment.""

"But…" Sadie spoke; fear has an antidote. All eyes turned to Sadie; "Love!" So, Sadie sang, "All You Need Is Love, love, love is all you need!"

"Got that right," Chris laughed. And, girl, we love you!"

Following Chris' lead, they left their place in the circle to surround Angel in a group hug.

"I hope that all this fear business is over for you, Angel," Mia said.

"Not quite," Angel answered, "between my Mom, Ms. Foster, the just in case clause, and LOVE, I'm sure, I'll get past this.

"I know you will," Mia answered. "Being the leader of a mission can be rough. I know. Remember how I acted. Seems to me, the mission is not only for the person you are assigned to but, well somehow it's a mission for you as well."

"You know," Angel replied, "I never thought about it that way, but you do have a point. All I know for sure is, I'm so glad to have each one of you as my friend!"

"But there is one other thing," Angel said. "Remember, I was telling you all about that older woman that helped me when I ran away from the Sanctuary? The girls nodded.

"Well, what I didn't tell you, I saw her again when I went to visit Taylor at the hospital. I left Taylor because I got upset with her. I was fuming, and I guess I was talking out loud because out of nowhere, she answered. Bout scared the life out of me. Anyway, she gave some excuse that she was sitting on the bus stop a short distance away. I know I was upset, but I'm sure, if she had been at that bus stop, I would have seen her. Angel stopped, catching her breath. "That's not the only thing, when she left, well let's just say it was real…strange. What do you think, Ms. Foster?

"Again, Angel," Eve exclaimed. "Here you go with that strange woman story!"

"Yeah," Chris joined in; "Someone get this girl something to drink.

"No, seriously," Angel replied. "There really was something strange about her."

"You know Angel," Mia answered. "You need something to take your mind off seeing strange old women. I've got an idea. Let's all sound off, you know the way we did that night we named ourselves the God Squad. Ready go…"

Ms. Foster sat back in her chair, a frown creasing her brow as she contemplated what Angel had said. With a sigh, she watched as the girls stepped forward, seeing each clad in their spiritual armor.

I'm Angel,
I go into battle wearing the Shoes of the Gospel of Peace. When I stand up and plant my feet, first right then left, a whole lot of shakin goes on around me but I can stand firm and not fall for the lies and deceit the giants bring my way.

I'm Chris,
I never go into battle without the Breastplate of Righteousness. It guards my heart and keeps me strong, even against giants.

Everything, I believe is in my heart and the breastplate keeps it pure so when I speak my words are like laser beams, accurate and true.

I'm Sadie,
To defeat the giants, I have the Belt of Truth. I buckle it up around my waist before going into battle and when the giants try to catch me up in their web of lies and deceit...I just whip off the Belt of Truth and... zap em!

I'm Jade,
Giants are no match for me when I put on the Helmet of Salvation. Mind, clear and focused, attentive to God's leading and direction, all the static of the enemy is stopped, and I can advance forward in the battle assured of victory.

I'm Eve,
Giants don't stand a chance against the Shield of Faith. I go into battle with the assurance that whatever fiery darts are hurled at me, I just put up my Shield and let the blinding light of faith shine forth and watch the flames disappear.

Hey, guys, don't forget about me!

I'm Mia,
Don't even think about going into battle without the Sword of the Spirit. The Sword can cut off any scheme, plot, or plan just like I did with the giants. So, take your power stand, pick up your sword and swoosh, cut the enemy off.

Wow, that was some mission! Hope you enjoyed going along with the God Squad as they took on another Mission Him-Possible.

We learned about some important lessons in this adventure. Bullying is not girls being girls, or boys being boys for that matter.

Bullying is awful!

I hope you will remember that if you are being bullied, tell someone. If you are afraid, like Taylor, Sarah, or even me, find someone you can trust and TALK ABOUT IT!

If you know someone that you suspect is being bullied. Be a friend. reach out to them. Bullying is a scary thing and can end up being dangerous. The only way bullying is going to stop is for you to stop it. Ignoring it or hoping it will go away does nothing.

Bullying creates a lot of other emotional challenges. For me it was anger, fear, and shame. I couldn't have gotten through the emotional fall-out of bullying without the help of my mentor and counselor, Ms. Foster. I hope you will remember, you are not a whimp to ask for help. Some things you just cannot get through by yourself. And, that's okay. We all need help some time or another.

Remember, you don't have to fear the giants because you know the Giant Slayer! From me and the other members of the God Squad, may each day you be transformed by the Word, empowered by the Holy Spirit, covered with Prayer Power, and dressed for every battle in the full Armor of God!

Angel

You can learn more about us by going to our website:

www.godspecialforces.com

See where the God Squad and Mission Him-Possible got started in: "Mission Him-Possible I, the Distorted Mirror."

Available at:

Amazon.com

Would you like to be a member of the God Squad? Log on to www.godspecialforces.com

Follow the instructions and complete the questionnaire for becoming a member of the God Squad.